Dedicated to my children

Stephanie
Sara
Michael

and my grandchildren

Bella
Brie
Sebastian

In memory of my mother

Isabelle Sant' Ambrogio

WOMEN RISING

John Sant'Ambrogio

ISBN 978-1-943650-52-1

This book available though amazon.com
and all online bookstores.

Published by BookCrafters, Parker, Colorado.
www.bookcrafters.net

CHAPTER

1

AN OMINOUS VISITOR

While the Carters made supper, Steve stood next to his wife Annie and noticed she seemed taller, as beautiful as ever, but taller. She wasn't wearing her high heels so he couldn't understand what was going on. And her clothes looked so tight.

He laughed, *I can't be shrinking, can I?*

Lately he noticed she was eating much more than usual. After dinner they relaxed in their beautiful big living room and watched the CBS news. Several scientists were interviewed about their analysis of a strange meteor-like sphere that had recently circled the globe and shocked everyone and how it was affecting human beings. Actually, just women. A prominent Harvard scientist echoed the opinion of many other experts. He felt the sphere's vibrations affected feminine DNA, but not men's, all over the country and perhaps the world. Women's appetites were increasing and their bodies were growing taller and stronger.

Steve and Annie looked at each other and Steve said, "Annie, can you stand up next to me for a second? Let's go in front of a mirror." They both were shocked. There was no doubt that Annie had really risen in height just recently. After they measured her they realized she was now 5'9", an increase of four inches in three weeks from her previous 5'5". Steve hugged Annie because he could see she was very frightened. She was in tears.

"Oh dear, oh dear, I thought something was happening to me, but I just tried to ignore it."

In fact, that was what most people had been doing, but now that the truth was out, ignoring was just ignorance, and very important questions were being asked by everyone: "When will this effect cease, and could it be harmful?"

Three months later doctors and scientists had come to the conclusion that there were no harmful effects from the vibrations. However, the growth in women had not ceased. In fact it was increasing measurably. Women were becoming so much stronger. They were actually getting stronger and taller than most men. The world was in turmoil, and the news focused on watching and waiting. When was this unbelievable growth syndrome going to end?

Then it happened. Six months after the strange vibrations entered the earth's atmosphere, the effect on women's bodies stopped. Most women were now so much taller than they were before the sphere's effect. Girls in school were teased and called giants. The women's clothing industry skyrocketed, although woman's high heels were now out of fashion. The demand for bigger women's shoes rivaled the demand for higher heeled men's boots. Grocery stores struggled to meet the new food demand. It was a different world, and the next chapter was about to begin.

CHAPTER

2

CRAZY CHAOS

The six months after the sphere's visit were perhaps the most turbulent times in the history of mankind. Actually, no one knew what to think. While women's abnormal growth had continued, most of the world had not started to contemplate what this change in the human species was going to mean for civilization. One would guess this was because everyone was in shock. People were simply blown away by the changes that were happening to the ladies and were fearful that it was never going to stop. Studies had shown that all women had grown taller by two feet or more. However, all the ramifications of this phenomenon had not been considered quite yet.

Then everything changed. The scientists announced that after examining all the recently gathered data from around the world, they felt confident saying the strange growth syndrome in women had finally ended. There was a sigh of relief all over the world. But the world would need more than a sigh of relief.

One evening during supper Steve sensed sadness on Annie's face. "Annie I love ya. Even though you're two feet taller than me and we had to spend so much money on new clothes for you," he said teasingly. "Your size has nothing to do with my love for you. I love you for who you are. Your new body hasn't changed all those wonderful feminine qualities of warmth and tenderness you show me and everybody else. And oh yes, your gorgeous blonde hair still knocks me dead. It hasn't changed a bit. Maybe a little thicker," he joked. "And I just love your incredible beautiful long eye lashes."

"Steve, I don't know how I could survive this without you. You are the true man. Can I give you a hug?"

"Sure, just don't squeeze me too hard, you almost broke a rib last night," Steve kidded. "Remember, I'm kinda skinny." Annie got up and hugged Steve and kissed him on the top of his head. It was obvious she was not happy with what was happening.

This didn't seem to be the case with her friend and neighbor, Jane Porter. Jane was thrilled with her new size. Although the Carters and the Porters both believed families should consider themselves teams, Jane's husband, Bob, felt he was the quarterback. In fact he looked like one with his broad shoulders and muscular arms. He was considered tall and handsome in spite of his graying hair, and he was really strong, too. He loved Jane deeply, but he felt it was his job and even his right, to order her and their two girls around, making all the important decisions for the "family" on his own. On the other hand their neighbors Steve, who never ordered anyone around, and Annie seemed to feel they were playing mixed doubles. Their team was a partnership of equality.

Unlike Annie, Jane, with her new very long dark hair and beautiful bright smile, loved the fact that she had grown so much taller and was now even stronger than Bob. This physical change to all women reinforced the power of the women's movements.

"Wait Bob, I'll move the breakfront so we can dine more comfortably at the dining room table. Just keep stirring the stew."

"Jane, please stop ordering me around," Bob pleaded. "You make me feel like a little kid."

"Well, you are little in size compared to me," replied Jane with a playful grin.

Obviously bewildered, Bob answered with a troubled look, "None of this makes sense! It's not right. What's happened to the caveman theory?"

Jane laughed, "The cave woman theory has taken over I guess." Then as a second thought she said, "Bob, since I'm now stronger than you, perhaps you can learn how to cook, get the kids properly dressed in the morning, drive them to school, clean the house... And, I could take over your job shipping and handling supplies at the plant."

"Jane, how can you talk like this? Are you kidding? They would never hire you."

"Really? Last week I secretly had an interview

with them about a job, and they were really excited about my application. My almost seven foot height and super strength would allow me to load far more material faster than men – even than you! They were so excited that they offered me a higher salary than yours, but I thought I should be fair and talk with you first. Hey did you hear that? Me talk with you first before making a 'family' decision. When was the last time we did that?"

Bob was quiet and then asked, "What's going on here? What am I supposed to do now?" Finally he softly muttered, "Since I'm the quarterback I guess I should decide what to do next."

"Bob, you always said we were a team and you were the quarterback. Now that I'm so much bigger and stronger than you I could be tempted to make myself the quarterback, but no, I'm going to say we are a mixed doubles team. Let's work this out together."

Bob was again quiet. Finally he said, "Jane if our income is going to increase I guess we should let you go to work at the plant, and maybe we can buy a bigger house like the Carters on the hill that overlooks a beautiful California meadow. But I don't want to do all those things you've been doing."

"Oh yeah? Who is going to do them?"

Bob was really upset, and he looked so sad Jane could see it was probably best if she stopped lecturing him. She sensed he was very troubled. "Don't worry Bob, we'll get some paid help, and we can both work."

But Bob did not perk up. He was not happy to realize they were both going to have the same job, and Jane was going to be paid more for her work then he was. Bob was unhappy, but Jane was not.

Next door Annie was really down. The only thing keeping her going was her husband's comforting love that he continually expressed. Each morning he hugged Annie and told her, "Annie you look so beautiful; you are so majestic, so beautiful. Your height doesn't take anything away from your glorious being, but watch your head by the fan. Maybe we should use a floor fan to keep us cool."

Annie wiped tears from her eyes and gently returned Steve's hug. "That talk show last night on CBS really brought to light the traumas we are facing in this country; in fact in the entire world. On one hand, I guess some of the women, though certainly not all, in Saudi Arabia are quite happy about the situation. Most Saudi women liked things just the way they were before the sphere's visit and are so unhappy with the turn of events, but some have told their husbands they were going to drive whether they liked it or not. Former masters are reported feeling so intimidated by the size of the women that they give them the car keys. So I guess things aren't all bad. But Steve, I hate it. I can't stand it."

"Honey, I understand. I don't know if this will make you feel any better but look what's happening in the inner cities. Remember what we heard last week on the news? That psychologist, Raymond Bates, claimed fewer husbands were running away because women's superior strength enabled them to prevent their partners from leaving. They often searched them out after they tried to desert them, grabbing them and pulling them back to their apartments and telling them, 'You ain't going anywhere! You're gonna take care of the kids 'cause I got a job'."

Annie sorta smiled and added, "And studies show wife abuse is disappearing, and rape doesn't seem to exist or be an issue anymore. I know sexual abuse in colleges has ceased. But, Steve, don't make me feel guilty. I know all these facts and they certainly are helping some women — but not me. I loved it when you were able to pick me up and twirl me around."

Steve interrupted, "Honey we can still do that." He then ran over, picked Annie up and started to twirl her around. Unfortunately he didn't realize how long Annie's beautiful legs were, and they knocked over the precious old flower pot on the coffee table, breaking the pot. Annie was so heavy, Steve fell down, and she practically crushed him when they landed on the floor.

"See what I mean, Steve? With this terrible new body I'm so afraid, when I cuddle with you in bed, I might crush you when I put my arm on top of you."

"Annie, I know. I understand, but just because you can't put your arm on top of me, it doesn't mean we can't sleep next to each other and be close."

Annie sighed, and Steve whispered, "Dear One, it's not your size or strength or even your beauty that defines you. Love defines you. You express love now as you always did. I saw you help our older neighbor the other day. You ran out and helped him unload all the wood from his truck. That was so kind of you."

Annie replied, "I had to...he used to do things like that for me."

Steve butted in, "And your size hasn't stopped you from being a great editor for our local paper."

Just then there was a knock on their door, "Steve, I think our wonderful neighbors the Porters are here."

Steve rushed to the door and gave Bob and Jane hugs. He warned Jane to watch her head coming in the door. She ducked and followed Bob into the living room.

"Well, I brought the salad with delicious pineapple again."

"Thanks Jane. The chicken is almost done on the barbecue."

"Great, I'll go out with Annie to help finish the cooking."

Bob slumped on the sofa with a downcast face, "How are you putting up with this mess?"

"Oh, I guess it's a mixed blessing. I'm bearing it. How about you Bob?"

"I'm not bearing it."

Steve felt for Bob and paused. He wanted to say something upbeat, hoping to change Bob's mood, "Well, as we have all been hearing on the news and talk shows, I guess some problems in the world seem to be getting resolved, and it's helping the women's movements too."

"Yeah, that's what a lot of people are saying. Not that I don't care about others, but this is a disaster for me, and I don't know how I'm going to deal with it. I was born a man. Men have always been the leaders. Look what's happened at the ballet — now women are tossing the men around! It's almost like Jane wants to toss me around, and she's trying to be the leader in our family. I don't care if she is seven feet tall, she can't be the leader. I cant stand this role reversal. Men have been in control for thousands of years and women have been in their right place — under us."

All this made Steve uncomfortable. He and Bob had never had a discussion like this before. Steve didn't want to start an argument and spoil the evening, especially because Annie had been counting on this get-together to raise her spirits. However, Steve's lawyer skills were forcing him to step forward.

"Bob, before this crazy thing happened, weren't many women starting to be treated more equally, at least in our country? Maybe this sphere is teaching us something."

"What?" Bob asked.

At that moment Jane and Annie burst from the kitchen and yelled, "Supper is ready." Steve was grateful for the interruption in their debate. In spite of being a successful lawyer, Steve didn't like testy arguing. Unlike some lawyers, he just wasn't the arguing type, and he had a lot of humility.

CHAPTER

3

THE RUNAWAY

After their delicious supper the Porters and the Carters and their lovely kids gathered in the living room to watch CNN. The president was addressing the nation to talk about all the challenges the U.S. faced during these difficult times. Of course, the U.S. was not the only nation perplexed by the sphere's visit to the earth. There were so many factions fighting each other, the president felt called upon to try to calm the nation.

"My fellow Americans, these are trying times for us, and I urge us all to have patience with each other. No one could have foreseen this situation, so, I urge everyone to be patient and have compassion for each other."

This was one of the few times Jane and Steve agreed but for different reasons. Jane was so happy with the turn of events. She was enjoying the fact that she could finally take over the quarterback position, even though she knew it wouldn't happen overnight. She thought,

Great, I hope everybody takes time to make decisions. I don't want to see us rush into this. Time will let everyone finally come to the obvious conclusion, which is women should be the bosses. If we push too fast, the men will fight us like crazy as they always do. We need patience as the president is suggesting.

The president finished his speech, "Many are still in shock at what has happened, so as I have previously said, we must be compassionate with each other and be patient. For as the Bible tells us, 'All things work together for good, for those who love God.' We can handle this challenge by working together."

Steve agreed with the president, but he did not agree with what he knew Annie was thinking, "now women are superior." He felt, as he always had, that size and strength did not determine who we were or who should be in control. He believed no one should think they were superior. Steve had always been supportive of women.

Once the president finished his speech the kids wanted to watch the NFL football game, Cardinals vs. Packers. Sports had always been one of the more popular events on TV, but now they were the most watched programs. Why? Men's pro teams in all sports were stealing women from the women's teams, even basketball teams!

One example was eight foot tall Rachel Good who had been playing basketball since she was a kid. She was a star on the "Cats," the leading women's pro team, but now she played for the Lakers. Because of her size she didn't have to jump to dunk the ball. The fans loved the changes, but the women's team owners were furious. All kinds of law suits were filed, and the game wasn't over.

Some women's teams were trying to arrange games with men's teams before they lost too many players. It was turmoil, but the fans loved it. And football! Oh my! Women wore huge chest guards, but that didn't stop them from reaching over the heads of their opponents and intercepting passes.

Seventeen year old Susie and fifteen year old Sara Porter squealed with delight as the two families watched the game, but eighteen year old Paul and sixteen year old Peter Carter were not as excited or happy about what they saw. "Look at those arms on Dorothy Pence. She must really work out!" Susie shouted.

Peter and Paul were quiet. The kids were great friends, but now the boys felt intimidated. This new atmosphere was created in high schools across the country, and boys and girls were more separated than they had been in the past.

"Okay kids, time for bed," Jane announced.

After the children left, the Carters and Porters sat in the living room. Bob quietly offered his gratitude for their company. "Thank you for who you are. In spite of this travesty and the fact we may see things differently, we are still friends. But I'll be honest, this whole mess makes me want to stop living."

The Carters and Jane were aghast. No one said a word, but their faces showed their shock. Bob stood and walked out. He didn't go home, but walked through the neighborhood hoping to lose his deeply depressed feelings as he viewed the lovely clear night with the beautiful stars and the gorgeous full moon. Stunned, Jane, Annie and Steve quietly looked at each other.

Annie was the first to speak, "I share his feelings, but of course for different reasons. This has been a shock to each of us. None of us knows who we really are anymore."

"Well, I have to say, I don't much mind being someone different," Jane commented. "For years I have been the servant, the second in command. Bob never pushed me around, but because he towered above me and would hover over me when he ordered me to do things, I often felt intimidated, but not anymore. Now his tune has changed. It's more like he's asking as he looks up to me. I never liked feeling that I was being talked down to. It's kinda fun to talk down to him now."

"Well, apparently many women are delighted with what's happened," Annie jumped in, "but I don't like it at all." She left and went upstairs.

Jane shouted after her, "Oh Annie, I'm so sorry." She picked up the Scrabble board and went home.

The next morning Jane returned before Annie left for her job at the local newspaper. Jane was crying.

"Annie, Bob never came home last night. He hasn't called, and he doesn't answer his cell phone. I called the plant and they say he never showed up for his early shift. The plant is really pushing me to work for them. I'm gonna have to sign up now that Bob has disappeared." Jane sobbed. "At least I'm grateful my daughter Susie is old enough to drive. But oh, I miss Bob so much, and I'm worried he's ended his life."

"This is terrible! So you called him on his cell?"

"Yes, but he doesn't answer. I'm not even sure he still has it. I've called the police to let them know what's happened. Lord forgive me, I was too hard on him."

Annie hugged Jane and tried to comfort her. "Jane, this is not your fault. This is the sphere's fault. In some ways it's our society's fault. If we had been more compassionate and patient with each other, as the president begged us to be, maybe we wouldn't be going through all this."

Steve came down the stairs and saw the sad scene in the living room, "What's going on? Did Bob settle down last night? What's wrong?" The ladies were still holding each other, and Steve sensed what had happened. "Oh my goodness. So Bob never came back home last night? I'll call the office and tell them I have an emergency."

This was not an ideal time. His office was loaded with tons of cases. There were all kinds of legal disputes caused by the sphere's visit, but Steve knew he had to help his neighbor before anything else.

"Jane, I'll start driving through the north end of town and you and Annie deal with the south end."

After driving for hours all over town, checking with the police and sending out hundreds of emails to all their friends, they hadn't been able to find a trace of Bob.

The next day Annie posted a notice in the paper about Bob's disappearance, but a week later, there was still no sign of him and no word from the police. Annie and Steve did all they could to comfort Jane and her daughters. Peter and Paul helped too. Seeing Susie and Sara cry eased their feelings of intimidation. As more and more time passed everyone feared, considering how depressed Bob was, he might have ended his life. But something would happen that would surprise them all.

CHAPTER
4

A CHANGED MAN

Six weeks after Bob disappeared, Jane received a letter from him. She ran to the Carters to joyfully share it with them. They sat on the sofa while Jane read Bob's letter out loud to them.

Jane, forgive me for leaving you and not letting you know where I was. I was so depressed that I was tempted to end my life, and then I met some men who were in the same boat as I was. As I put my sadness aside for a moment, I began to find some joy helping others to cope with the problem of feeling inferior like I did.

As I met more and more men challenged the same way as I was, I came up with an idea to form an organization devoted to helping men deal with the recent events. I'm calling it MM.

Annie quipped, "He must mean AA...M&Ms sound like candy."

No, it's Merciful Men," Jane explained. Then she went on with the letter.

I have formed MM as an organization to help men like me, men who have been so shocked by this change in their lives, that they have come close to mental breakdowns. The meetings help us deal with the fact that we no longer are the 'big guys in town.' I think most of us have had to give up our chauvinistic tendencies. I know I did. If this crazy thing hadn't happened I'm not sure if I ever would have changed. So Jane, I hope you will forgive me. If you want I can come back home, because I think I'm getting better at dealing with this disaster.

As they read the last word of his letter there was a knock on the front door. Steve ran over and opened it and there was Bob, standing still. He didn't look like himself. He had a big beard and moustache, and he had a slight smile on his face. Everyone ran over to hug and kiss him. Jane, shouting with joy, was able to wrap her huge arms around Bob and the Carters.

Steve, realizing how important this moment was for the Porters and how they needed to spend time alone with each other said, "What a blessing this is from the Lord. Let's all say good night and let our dear friend return to his home, where he'll be so welcomed."

Later Steve shouted from the bathroom, "I'd love to

know what that MM organization Bob started does to help men as troubled as he was. How do they deal with the present crazy world?"

"I'd like to know, too," answered Annie, "Maybe I can start my own WW self-help group. Let's see, maybe 'Worried Women' or 'Wonderful Women'."

Steve added with a laugh, "Or 'Wimpy Women'."

"No," Annie countered, "'Wishy Washy Women' is better."

They both laughed as Steve turned out the light. The joking lifted Annie's spirits, and before they fell asleep she added, "Or maybe Bob would let me join his group and help men and women work together to deal with this mess."

The next day the news said terrorist organizations all over the world were in turmoil because women were rebelling. Apparently they were joining together in groups, grabbing men's weapons and refusing to abide by the commands of the caliphate leaders.

Steve said to Annie as she fixed breakfast, "Wow, this worldwide change certainly has affected the Middle East."

"I know," Annie answered, "there's no question that this has brought some good to the world, but not to me. I know I shouldn't complain, but I'm still unhappy personally. I want to be who I was and not who I am."

"Annie," Steve reassured her, "remember what I keep telling you. Your size has not changed the way I see you, and it never will."

At breakfast the next day Jane asked Bob, "What is the message of the MMs?"

"Well, Jane, we don't have just one message. There are many, but one thing that united us was that we all need to understand who we really are. We have to learn that we're not just big or small, not just good looking or a little less than good looking, not just young or uh ...maybe mature. No, we need to see the important fact that we're more than big or small, red or green in a physical body. We found that when we recognized ourselves spiritually rather than materially, we saw a different path to follow. We had felt so intimidated by the new size of you ladies that our self-esteem fell through the floor. And when we realized we couldn't grow in size, we began to see that we could grow in character. We decided to remember that before all this happened, women asked to be treated equally. So we didn't have to feel guilty for asking the same thing, right?" Bob laughed at his sarcasm.

"Oh my goodness, Bob, you're blowing me away. What made you buy into all this? It doesn't sound like you at all."

Bob began, "Honey, it..."

But Jane interrupted him, "Bob, what's going on here? I used to call you 'honey' all the time, but you never ever called me that."

"I know. I guess one of the things we're learning is to be more affectionate to our wives even though they can push us around now."

Jane quickly jumped in, "Bob, that sounds a little passive aggressive."

"You're right. The truth is, I'm calling you 'honey' because I love you. Even if you do push me around, I'll still call you 'honey,'" he laughed. "I used to push you around and you still called me 'honey.' Anyway, the real reason is that it's a term of endearment."

Jane sat down and pondered what was going on. She couldn't take it all in. She didn't know whether or not to believe him. Was this the real Bob?

Next door, Annie woke up early, troubled, and started thinking about Bob. How did he handle his depression? She thought she was the only one depressed, but now she knew that wasn't true. Last night CNN had a whole hour devoted to the challenges facing so many women. *Many of us apparently don't want to be superior or inferior,* she thought. *Maybe we should start a WW group, like 'Wise Women,' or maybe 'Wonderful Women' or 'Women Winning.' No, that would just scare the men.*

Steve interrupted Annie's thoughts as he rolled out of bed. "Good morning dear. You seem to have awakened early this morning."

"Yes, I've been thinking about Bob."

"Me too. It's wonderful that he's back safe and sound. Would you help me carry that heavy old sofa out to the street so the junk truck can pick it up this morning?"

Annie nudged him. "Take a look out the window, Steve."

"Oh my gosh, it's out there already. Who'd you get to help you?"

"No one. I moved it myself last night. I knew they come early to pick up and I didn't want it taking up space in the garage for another week."

Steve was stunned. "Annie, how..."

"Well, as I said, things aren't all bad," Annie chuckled. "I know that the few times I come out of my gloom seem to be when I have the most strength to help others. And it's fun when I get something done that a man couldn't do before. I've decided to talk with Bob today to see if he'd let some women in his club."

"Go for it," Steve yelled over his shoulder as he headed for the office.

Three months later the former MM group had evolved into the huge MWT organization which now included both men and women in Merrydale, where the Porters and the Carters lived. This wonderful support organization had over 50,000 members all over the country, and was dedicated to helping men and women deal with the shocking changes that had occurred around the world. The Porters and Carters, working together, had originated, organized and were now leading the amazing MWT, the Men & Women Together organization. Women's groups were very supportive of MWT.

Bob, president, and Annie, vice-president, started this amazing group. But not everything was good. A great challenge was lurking nearby.

Annie and Bob were becoming heroes world-wide. In the U.S. they were celebrities. The president met with them and praised all they had done. Even the Pope, along with several seven and eight foot nuns, invited them for a glorious meeting in Rome. Frequently news and TV talk shows gave them opportunities to publicize their vision. And what was their vision? What was the message of the MWTs?

The message was that the important things in life were not physical strength and size, but the amount of love, compassion, kindness, tenderness and wisdom one expressed, that counted. Forget traditional standards of who was the biggest and strongest, your ethnic background, gender or what your religion was. Many of the world's religious leaders were getting on board with such a message. All seemed to be going very, very well. But something quite terrible was about to happen.

CHAPTER

5

TWO POINTS OF VIEW

Although many throughout the world were in agreement with Bob and Annie, there were also many who were passionately opposed to their views. Soon there was another organization being secretly formed in Merrydale, and it too was spreading around the country. They called themselves the TGs, or Tough Guys. Their hatred for Bob and Annie and what they were doing motivated Soapy Strong, a corporate CEO, to gather many of his like-minded buddies together in order to talk about the mess they felt they were in, especially the men. You might say they enjoyed being called chauvinistic. They rejected the idea of "let's live with it" or "if we are sweet and nice, they won't push us around." They stuck with "we men are still the bosses."

And believe it or not, many women were joining the TGs. They sort of enjoyed being ordered around. They weren't comfortable being bosses, and they liked staying home and welcoming their bread-winner husbands when they returned after a day at work. After all, that work supported the family and being taken care of was great. Who else but women could take care of the home? They liked focusing on being mothers and loving housewives. And who needed all the pressure of going out to compete for jobs? This new idea of changing women's roles seemed terrible to them. "Just leave us alone," was their motto. "Besides, this size advantage could just be fleeting."

Soapy could see what was happening all around him. He knew many who would accept his approach to deal with the chaos. He had his secretary print flyers and gave them to his friends and employees to distribute to their friends. Within a month he had attracted over six hundred men and women to his weekly meetings in an abandoned church. Soon other TG groups started throughout the land. All members pledged to keep silent about plans and ideas discussed at the meetings, and all were required to sign strict privacy contracts.

In spite of the rapid growth of TG, MWT was probably gaining the most public support. One problem was the TGs were not getting much news coverage and few invitations to appear on talk shows. They were getting a little press, but it wasn't always too helpful. One editorial labeled them unfairly as the new Klu Klux Klan. At TG's next Tuesday evening meeting, a discussion was held to address the lack of opportunities to get their message out and the need for more publicity.

Jeff Monty said, "Look, one of the reasons MWT is doing so well is Bob Porter's charisma. In spite of the shock and confusion created by that horrible sphere, he is succeeding in reaching people. The truth is everyone is uncertain about what we should be doing. How do we face the new female giants and amazons? Bob was the first to offer a solution. And even if it's not a good one, people think his approach is great. But Soapy, you have more charisma than Bob. So let's get you out there."

Immediately the six hundred men and women rose to their feet and yelled with enthusiasm, "Yeah, yeah, hooray."

Three days later Fox News agreed to bring Bob and Soapy together for a Sunday morning debate.

Jane questioned Bob's willingness to meet and debate Soapy.

"Bob, do you really think this is wise? Why should you even give him the opportunity to appear on TV with you?"

Bob responded, "Honey, he's already started to go on TV and other talk shows, and frankly I don't think the commentators are really questioning him in ways that reveal the dark side of TG's philosophy of male superiority. TG now seems to be coming out of its secretive mode, and its lies need to be countered. I'm hoping I can start the process that needs to occur to get the truth out. Our country, before the effect of the sphere's invasion, would have labeled his philosophy as crazy misogyny. But the unbelievable disaster that has hit us has knocked us unconscious. We don't know what to think or how to think. You know the mental challenges Annie and I went through, and millions of other men and women are experiencing the same feelings we had.

"I feel it's urgent that we be there for everyone. We must help them get through this mess as Annie and I did. There are just so many undecided voters – just like before the 2016 election. Remember how the debates changed the outcome that November? We need to stop this crazy movement in its tracks and not let it get its roots in the soil."

"Maybe you are right, honey, probably we shouldn't let the TGs get overconfident because of their success," Jane finally agreed.

About 7:00 p.m. Saturday there was a knock on Soapy's door. It was Jeff Monty, an enthusiastic TG member.

"Oh, hi, Jeff," Soapy greeted. "What's up?"

"Soapy, someone has talked to me privately about wanting to do something drastic to stop the terrible MWT's growth. I promised to keep it a secret, but I feel I have to tell you."

"What do they want to do, Jeff?"

"Take down Bob."

There was silence. "Jeff that is absurd. I never heard what you just said. Go tell your friend he should forget it."

At 8:30 Sunday morning, Bob and Soapy were backstage getting ready for their 9:00 a.m. debate. Ralph Master and Mary Reed were moderating, and they were putting together tough questions both Bob and Soapy would have to answer. Mary was 7'5" and Ralph was 5'11" so the stagehands had a very short chair for Mary and a very high stool for Ralph. Except for sports, TV directors were doing everything possible to hide the huge disparities in the sizes of men and women. It was possible that this debate was going to be one of the most exciting programs the ten million viewers were going to witness. At 9:00 a.m. Bob and Soapy walked into the studio and sat on their chairs.

Ralph began, "Good morning, gentlemen. We are happy to have you here this Sunday morning at a time the nation and the world are facing one of the greatest challenges in our history. We are hoping you will give us some ideas on how the human race can deal with these challenges."

Mary added, "You both lead fast growing organizations that help people cope with these challenges, though in totally different ways."

Then Ralph asked the first question. "Bob, why do you feel your groups have the right answers to deal with our dilemma?"

"Well, for one thing, I'm wondering if this dilemma is really teaching us some lessons. For thousands of years we have approached male and female relationships in a very biased way. It's been "the bigger the better" rule. The strongest is supreme, and women have had to struggle to be heard. Now that we face a situation where women are bigger and stronger than most men, we are forced to question the truth of the former theory."

Bob continued, "Does this mean men must now be subservient to women? That possibility has frightened and depressed many of us, both men and women. But when we take the physical out of the picture and focus on the many other wonderful qualities we all possess, our world changes. MWT feels that this is an opportunity for men and women to be equal, regardless of size and physical strength, something that has not been the case for centuries.

"I know that we think the sphere brought about these unbelievable changes to women, but actually before all this happened, many women were getting taller, often taking care of their husbands. Unfortunately, it didn't seem to have much effect on the way many men thought, and I was one of them. I had to change. So maybe this event needed to happen to wake us up. MWT is helping men and women deal with changes and return to peace and sanity, be filled with joy as they see the real kind man and the real tender woman. We try to not look at the physical bodies but rather look at wonderful spiritual qualities we all possess."

"Thank you, Bob," Mary spoke. "Soapy, how do you look at all this?"

Soapy couldn't wait to counter Bob's points. "If you study the Bible, you will find so much written about men being the leaders and given authority over women. Women are told to obey their husbands."

Annie, Jane and Steve watched the debate on TV in the Carters' living room and Steve complained, "Here goes Soapy, I just knew he'd bring the Bible in to try to win his case."

Soapy continued, "For thousands of years, it's been the men who have led the people and the nations. Once you give women equal power or, heaven forbid, supreme power, the world will be in chaos. Look what Delilah did to Sampson. Look what black widow spiders do to their mates. They kill them. With all the physical power women have now, they could soon betray us just like Delilah did. We must pass laws that will protect men.

"I know this might sound crazy to some, but maybe there should be better gun control. Perhaps women shouldn't be allowed to have guns. Now that they are so big and strong, they could hurt us if men didn't have guns for protection. Men have had supreme authority up to now and that brought us a long way. To be a great leader you must have the qualities of inner strength and courage. And most men have these qualities. Bob says to focus on the spiritual qualities. Well, men are the ones with the best spiritual qualities. Think of Moses and Jesus."

Ralph turned to Bob and asked, "What do you think of what Soapy claims?"

Bob answered, "Well if you were going to quote the Bible I would suggest some other quotes. In Genesis we learn that God created man, male and female, but I don't think God said one was supreme. It seems to me we are created equal, not one superior to the other. And in Galatians 3 it says, 'there is neither male nor female, for ye are all one in Christ Jesus.' I think that reinforces what I feel we are. We are more than just a male or female body.

"We should also remember that women, not men, were the ones who stayed with Jesus while He was on the Cross. And again it was women who discovered His empty tomb and announced His resurrection to the male disciples. There is no doubt that women played a very significant role in the Bible."

Back at the Carters, Steve yelled, "Hooray."

Bob continued, "I just feel that spiritual strength is possessed equally by both men and women. Actually, I feel we have to forget the physical body in order to grow spiritually."

Mary turned to Soapy. "Any more thoughts, Soapy?"

"I'm afraid I'm not convinced by Bob's comments. A lot of men I know wouldn't buy into his arguments. I think the proof of who's right will be determined by the future size of our organizations, the ones that gather the most people. By the way, we have both men and women in the TGs. There are lots of women who don't want to be superior or equal. They enjoy having men be in charge. They love to sit back and let the men be bold. It makes them feel safe."

Ralph ends the debate with a chuckle, "All right, we will see which grows the fastest, TG or MWT. Next month we'll check your attendance."

After the debate ended, Bob rushed to the Carters, He wanted to see how everybody thought he had done. As he walked in the front door, everybody cheered. They all hugged him, including their kids.

"You were great, Bob!" Steve shouted.

"You were right, Bob. I'm glad you agreed to do the show. I was wrong. Don't listen to me anymore, unless I order you to take out the garbage," Jane chuckled.

"Well, I'm so glad you thought I did well. Soapy is a tough smart guy. Now I just wanna relax and eat some barbecue chicken. Got any?"

Annie laughed, "Yup, we have some for you."

So the day ended on a high note, great food, love and friendship, and the belief MWT was winning the battle. Unfortunately, the battle had just begun.

CHAPTER

6

THE PLOT THICKENS

Soapy was not happy. His seven foot tall, soft-spoken wife, Mabel, tried to console him, but with no luck. Soapy sat down to eat the delicious dinner Mabel prepared for him.

"I can't stand that Bob. I sure hope the viewers didn't buy into his nonsensical diatribe. He's not right about anything. But he has a lot of charisma and it's helping him to build MWT. We gotta stop him. Mabel, what did you think about the debate?"

"Oh, I thought you did just fine, Soapy." Actually she didn't sound too enthusiastic, and Soapy got the message. After he finished eating, he gave Mabel a hug, thanked her for her support and went to bed.

The next day at the TG's board meeting everyone was furious. "Bob Porter is crazy. We gotta get rid of him," the members shouted. Soapy just looked sad and didn't say anything for a long time. Finally, when things quieted down, he spoke.

"Ladies and gentlemen, I ask you to ponder our challenges. We need to get out there and talk and talk and talk. We must tell our members to hand out our flyers and network with as many people as possible. When they see a giant woman with her normal sized husband, hand him the flyer. If they look at all interested, then take a few moments to chat with them."

Jeff interrupted and said, "Soapy, all your ideas are great, but we gotta take Bob down." The rest of the board nodded in agreement. Soapy dropped his head and then put up his hands, "No, no, we can't do that." Then he quickly walked out of the room. Like it or not, Soapy knew that a terrible seed had been planted.

Another organization incensed with the circumstances was the Mafia. Jeff had a friend in high school who was a member. After the TG board meeting, Jeff took out his cell phone. "Tony," Jeff spoke quietly on his phone. "Could we get together for some pasta tonight?"

"Sure," Tony answered with enthusiasm. Jeff had not talked with Tony for months and was elated they might get together again.

After dinner in a small Italian restaurant, Jeff started the conversation. "Tony, is it tough for you guys with all the women turning into monsters?"

"Jeff, it's hell. Many of the wives are bullying their husbands, believe it or not. So many are buying into that crap from Bob Porter. He's building such a huge gang of guys and dolls. That meeting Bob had with the Pope is cutting into our power. He's just a showman. Many of our guys are so confused, and they don't know what to do next."

"Tony, there is an answer."

"Really?" Tony responded with a puzzled look.

"The bad guy here is Bob Porter, and he has to be eliminated...and you guys can do it. Once he's gone, the MWT will shrink."

"Yeah, I think you're right. Let me raise the idea with the bosses."

Two days later Tony had an opportunity to speak with Giovanni, the top Mafia boss in Merrydale. "Giovanni, could we solve some of our problems if Bob Porter disappeared?"

"Yeah, Tony, we've been thinking about this for several weeks, and we have put together a great plan. One of our gang made contact with a young American called Madido who has become radicalized. He likes the idea of assassinating Bob for a radical terrorist group. Of course the stupid kid doesn't know that our guy Mr. X, who's been talkin' to him, is in the Mafia. He thinks Mr. X is just a terrorist sympathizer—you know how we sneak into every group in town. Our plan is to put the blame on terrorists, and of course they'll blame the Muslims."

"Wow, Giovanni, that's a great plan! When are we going to pull it off?"

"I can't tell ya, but it'll happen soon. And keep your mouth shut about it until then, or you won't live to see another day."

Tony left, promising to keep quiet and assuring Giovanni he had nothing to worry about.

CHAPTER

7

BETTER WATCH OUT, BETTER NOT CRY

MWT was growing by leaps and bounds. Bob was becoming more popular than a movie star, and Annie, as vice-president, was also gaining great notoriety. They were scheduled to speak together at a rally December 12th at the Town Hall. The auditorium had a capacity of over a thousand people and was expected to be sold out.

"The Town Hall meeting is the perfect setting for Madido to assassinate Bob," Giovanni told the bosses. "Get to Mr. X and tell him to buy Madido a ticket. Give him a pistol with a long barrel for accuracy. Mr. X should take him to the Town Hall a day early to check things out. And be sure the gun has no history so it can't be traced. Be sure Madido practices so he doesn't miss. Madido is willing to be caught and die for the radicals, and he believes he'll go to heaven and have seventy virgins. He thinks the terrorists will be proud of him."

While playing their weekly Scrabble game with the Carters, Jane said, "It's wonderful that you and Bob are going to be speaking together at the Town Hall rally. It shows how men and women can work together."

"That's true, Jane, we do work great together at MWT, but hey, be careful not to peek over at my Scrabble letters! Just 'cause you're tall and can see everything, that doesn't give you the right to cheat."

Jane yells out, "I wonder who has W R T S U M and an E." They all laughed.

"I'm told that more than a thousand are coming," Steve commented as he added up his score. He was the winner, but no one cared. They just loved getting together and never really competing, unlike their kids.

Jane called Susie and Sara who were in the basement playing mixed doubles ping pong with Peter and Paul. "Let's go girls, it's time for bed."

The kids rushed up the stairs, excited about the game they were playing. Because the girls were so big, playing mixed doubles was a challenge, and they had to be very careful not to hog the show. It was hard for Peter and Paul to squeeze in because Susie and Sara's long arms crowded them out. But they came up with a new rule that made it more fun for all of them. You had to stay on your side of the table, and if you reached over the middle, you lost the point. It made it more fun, and the boys didn't seem so intimidated.

Everyone shouted cheerfully as the Porters left for home. "See ya tomorrow at the Town Hall. Girls, watch your heads on the doors."

***

Madido arrived early the next day at the rally, so he could get a seat close to the stage. He found a center front row seat and knew it was perfect for what he was about to do. He was dressed in a dark suit, dark tie and white shirt, and his pistol was tucked in an inside coat pocket. He had a camera strapped around his neck. He didn't want to attract attention to himself, so he sat down and quietly pulled out a book he pretended to read. He didn't want to talk to anyone or be distracted. The audience began to fill the room, and two seven foot girls sat down on either side of him.

"Sir, would you move over one seat so we can sit next to each other?"

"No, I'm sorry I can't move because I'm taking pictures of the rally for our paper. This is exactly the right spot for me to catch them as they speak. But I won't be staying for all the speakers, so you can take my seat when I leave..." *or get killed by the police* he thought.

"Okay, we get it, but don't stay long," they chuckled softly.

When Annie and Bob walked on the stage there was a tumultuous roar from the crowd. They bowed, smiling, and sat down. Bob's chair was so tall it was a struggle for him to get up on it. Madido started to contemplate when would be the best time to shoot Bob. He reasoned if he let Bob speak too long it would allow him to spread more crap. But to his surprise, Annie and Bob walked to the edge of the stage and began to sing "Oh What a Beautiful Morning."

Madido was elated. *This is perfect. They're ten feet away and when they finish I'll shoot Bob when he bows.* Madido put his hand in his jacket, held onto the gun and planted his finger on the trigger. As they sang the last words of the song, Madido pulled out the gun and took careful aim at Bob. *The terrorists are going to call me a martyr. I'm gonna shoot Bob when they bow.*

Bob and Annie finished singing and took their bows as the crowd went wild. Betty and Barbara, the two giant girls sitting on either side of Madido, leaped into the air with joy. As they whipped their huge arms up to applaud, Barbara knocked the gun out of Madido's hand, and it fell on the floor. The amazons looked at each other in shock when they saw the gun Barbara had knocked out of Madido's hand. Then they looked at Madido, who was still pointing his hand at the stage.

They reached down, grabbed the dwarf by his arms and dragged him across the aisle. No one seemed to notice because the cheering crowd was wildly applauding Annie and Bob, who were bowing and smiling.

When the girls got to the lobby, they pulled Madido to the front doors and shoved him out. He landed hard on his belly. They closed the doors, ran back to their seats and grabbed the gun that nobody had noticed.

Barbara put the gun on her seat, and she sat on it. The audience finally calmed down, and Annie and Bob gave their great speeches.

When the rally was over and the stars left the stage, Betty and Barbara shouted for one of the ushers to come to them. When he reached them, they pointed at the gun and told him some idiot tried to shoot Bob, but they had knocked the gun out of his hand.

The usher was confused. "Why didn't you report what was happening to us or a policeman? What did you do with the alleged shooter?"

The girls knew they were in trouble. Betty answered, "One way or another he had to get outta here. We didn't want to interrupt the show or start a panic, so we grabbed him and threw him outta here."

"And," Barbara added, "since he was gone and the gun was on the floor, it seemed all right to wait until the rally was over."

The usher asked one of the police officers, who was also a giant woman, to talk with Barbara and Betty. The girls knew this wasn't going to be pretty. They were in trouble.

At the police station the girls were separated and put in different rooms. The interrogation began with Barbara. "Young lady, so far no one has reported that they saw a young man being dragged up the aisle in the middle of the rally. Are you denying that that gun was yours? We checked the fingerprints on the gun and found yours."

Barbara thought for a few seconds and prayed to

know what to say. She realized that all she could do was tell the truth and she knew Betty would do the same. So Barbara told everything that happened. The interrogator looked like he didn't believe her story and left the room. Betty told the truth as well, but the police didn't believe either of them. They were tossed in different cells.

Now they were really in trouble.

CHAPTER

8

MANIC MADIDO'S JOURNEY

A few days after the assassination attempt, Madido knew he was in trouble, too. *What does the terrorist supporter who gave me the gun think? I won't be a martyr. I'm a flop. I can't even go home. They'll find me and kill me, and I won't be a martyr.* As he passed a news stand he saw the headline in the paper.

TWO WOMEN ACCUSED OF ASSASSINATION ATTEMPT ON BOB PORTER

He was shocked. *This is not fair. They'll get all the credit from the terrorists.*

Back at the Porters, the two families were watching the news and were extremely upset at what they saw. It was said that two young women were being held for an attempt to murder Annie and Bob. During the commercial Jane said, "Bob, you can't do this anymore. You were almost killed by those two crazy women. You gotta quit!"

Steve piped in, "Bob and Annie, we've got to think deeply about this whole thing. I know you would hate to stop leading the wonderful movement you've created, but it looks like things are getting very dangerous."

After some silence, Bob spoke, "I can't stop fighting for equality for us all."

Annie quickly added, "Nor can I. And...I saw something last night that I didn't think much about till now."

"What?" they all cried out.

"I noticed two huge young women leading a little guy, who was sitting in front, up the aisle. I just thought it was three people who didn't like our singing, so I didn't pay much attention to what they were doing."

"Wow, we have to call the police immediately," Bob declared.

Annie went to the police station to report that what she had seen from the stage was exactly what Barbara and Betty claimed had happened. The two girls passed lie detector tests, and the police realized there were more prints on the weapon. Barbara and Betty were assured they would be released soon.

A search began for the young would-be assassin who had been thrown out of the Town Hall by the girls. The press published editorials that both praised and condemned the young ladies for the way they handled the situation. Bob and Annie praised the girls during press interviews.

In a TV interview, Bob made several points. "These two women saved Annie's and my life. They knew if they started screaming they might never have been heard over the noise of the crowd, and if they were heard, there could have been a stampede that would injure or even kill many people. They got this evil guy out of there, and no one was hurt. They have given a good description of the would-be killer, and he may soon be found."

Annie also stood up for the girls and told the press, "See, women having superior strength has paid off."

Other critics asked, "Why on earth didn't they just strangle him if they're so strong?"

***

Meanwhile Madido was living on the street, totally confused as to what to do next. *Maybe if I get credit for trying to kill Bob, the radical terrorists will take credit for my attempt, and I can die a martyr. I don't want to live anymore anyway, I'm so depressed.*

So Madido went to a library and wrote an anonymous note saying a man who matched Madido's description in the newspapers slept on a certain street. He printed it out and dropped it off at the police station. He ran out before anyone could grab him.

That night Madido was picked up and imprisoned. The next day Barbara and Betty identified him as the man they had thrown out of the Town Hall. Madido confessed to the crime.

Before Madido's confession was reported and it was

thought Betty and Barbara were guilty, Soapy had been delighted because there was new fuel for his campaign. "See, don't give guns to women. Look what they do with them. We men need more guns." Even the NRA had jumped on the bandwagon.

But now that the truth about what really happened was out, Soapy had to try a new approach in order to attract attention. So he joined the critics, who were furious over the fact that these big women had let the potential murderer go. "See, women don't know what to do. No man would ever have let the shooter go. Men are smarter."

Bob and Annie desperately wanted to support Barbara and Betty during this turmoil. They were so grateful for what the girls had done for them. The afternoon the ladies were to be released, Annie suggested, "Let's invite Betty and Barbara for dinner tonight and have them join our 'family'. It's the least we can do for them. They saved our lives!"

So the Porters and the Carters drove to the police station at twelve noon when the ladies were scheduled to be released. As the girls came out with their families, Bob walked up to them and said, "Ladies, we are so excited that you have been set free, and we would love to have you join us for dinner tonight."

"Oh, that is so kind of you," Barbara answered, "but we will be joyfully spending the evening with our parents."

"Bring them too," Steve said. "We have plenty of room for you all."

That evening the Porters and the Carters put on a fantastic party for twelve guests. The kids played their instruments for them after supper. Everyone felt so elated.

CHAPTER
9

BUSTING BOB

Madido was in jail, and it looked like everything was working out perfectly. Unfortunately, there was still trouble in the wind. Soapy was furious that Madido had been captured and the ladies were now being credited for saving Bob and Annie's lives. And worst of all, MWT was growing even bigger. The country was slowly being persuaded that size and strength were not as important as character and wisdom. Now MWT was even using the Bible! As Bob had previously done on the first TV debate, they quoted Genesis. "In the beginning God created man and woman, but I don't see where He said one was better than the other," Bob claimed at MWT's rallies. "And if we are going to quote the Bible, maybe there's no difference between men and women. In Galatians Paul writes "...in Christ we are neither male nor female."

But that did not persuade Soapy. "They are not equal to us," he shouted at his latest rally.

The crowd he attracted with his philosophy screamed, "Yeah, yeah, yeah." But as supportive as the crowds at his rallies were, they were getting smaller.

Later at the TG's board meeting Soapy commented, "We have to find some way to smear Bob. He's too perfect and his charisma is winning people over. Where are we going to be if things continue this way? We have to stop him."

Soapy's manager, Rusty, made a suggestion, "Maybe if we can find something in his past to shame him, people will stop joining him."

"Great idea," Soapy said, "but that might not be possible. Our researchers have determined he's pretty pure. Maybe we could tempt him with one of our beautiful long-legged women members, photograph him with her and get it into the papers."

From that moment on, TG's board began to concoct a scheme that they knew would bring Bob down. They were able to get Abigail Sony to join them. Along with the rest of the TG members Abigail, of course, disagreed with Bob's ideas, but she thought he was cute and charming. She imagined how great it would be to hug him.

"We need to spy on him," Rusty said. "Learn his schedule and find a time and place when he is alone, and then we can jump in and set something up. If we do it cleverly, he won't even know what we're up to." So that night they put together a brilliant plan.

After days of spying and following Bob, the TGs were able to locate a place he went each day that was isolated from the general public. Bob picked up his mail in the early evening at the post office and there was rarely anyone else there. The plan was simple. Just before Bob arrived at his usual time around 8:00 p.m., Abigail would lie on her back on the floor pretending to be gravely ill or wounded. They knew Bob was a compassionate guy and would immediately bend down to care for her. That would be the beginning of the show, and it would be Bob's end.

On Friday at 8:00 p.m., Bob went to his mail box, and there was Abigail lying on the floor on her back in a short skirt. She looked like the end was near. Her eyes were closed, and she moaned softly. Bob rushed over and bent down to help her, and Abigail whispered, "Sir, could you lift me up?" Because she was whispering so softly, Bob had to get close to her lips to hear what she was saying. "Could you put your arms under my shoulders and lift me up off the floor?"

As Bob leaned close to put his arms behind her huge shoulders, Abigail grabbed and held him tightly and then kissed him. She was so strong Bob couldn't pull himself away. Rusty and two other TGs rushed in and took photos of their embrace.

"What's this all about?" Bob shouted. Abigail jumped up laughing, and when Bob got up, she hugged him and rushed out of the room with the three men.

"Wait, wait. I wanna talk to you guys! Why did you do that?"

Bob realized what had just occurred, and he quickly left the post office and drove home. He ran into his house and exploded, "Jane, you won't believe what just happened! I think I was set up by some of Soapy's men at the post office to make it look like I was having an affair with some huge woman."

Jane laughed, "Oh Bob, there is no way anyone in their right mind is going to believe you did anything wrong." With Jane's help Bob calmed down, and they both laughed and went to bed.

The next day the pictures were in the papers, and they were so convincing that even Jane paused for a moment when she studied them. She wondered if it was really a set-up. The pictures showed a blanket under Abigail, and because they were enlarged and cropped, you couldn't tell where they were taken. But Jane quickly changed her mind and knew in her heart that it was a set-up to destroy Bob and MWT.

Soon Abigail was on TV saying Bob was her long-time boyfriend. Bob of course disclaimed the TG's propaganda. MWT faced the worst challenge in their short history.

At their weekly dinner at the Carters, Barbara and Betty, who were now a part of the "family", listened as Steve lamented about the mess Soapy created. "There is no question that this is a terrible scheme thought up by the TGs to discredit you, Bob."

Bob answered, "It has already cut our membership numbers. I know we have to find a way to get the press to see the true facts. But actually, what worries me the most is the guilt that Abigail must be feeling. She gave me one friendly hug before she left, and I feel that she was forced into doing this."

That night Bob pondered the whole situation before he went to sleep. Brilliant as he was, he could not come up with a solution. However, one thing kept coming to mind. More than fearing what might happen to MWT, he felt deeply for Abigail who might have been forced into being part of this scheme.

CHAPTER
10

THE TRUTH COMES OUT

The next day, while being interviewed by CNN, Bob again denied that there was any credibility to the incident. He felt moved to reach out to Abigail. "Dear Abigail, I'm sure you must know what you are claiming is not true, but I forgive you. You were either forced into creating the incident or were convinced by some group to be part of the scheme. You are not the guilty party here, and I forgive you."

Abigail was watching the broadcast at her apartment and was so touched by Bob's comments she was blown away. She was alone and had some quiet time to contemplate the situation. She was pretty convinced of the TG's "man is the top" philosophy. She had a domineering father who ordered her around, but always provided for her. However, she was beginning to admire Bob as a person. She felt so guilty. She fell into a deep depression.

After a restless night with little sleep, Abigail became convinced she had to tell the truth, no matter what philosophy she had bought into. She realized that once she spoke the truth, she was going to have to go into hiding. She went to the local TV station to find out how she might be able to make a true statement about what really did happen in the post office.

The staff went crazy when she came into the studio, and they quickly prepared to take videos of her when she recanted her story. The staff was so excited when they realized they would draw fantastic attention. They contacted their lawyers to witness the disclaimer.

Abigail testified that she had lied during a previous broadcast and that she had been persuaded to be part of a scheme. But she would not state who was behind the scheme, because she feared for her life. Once the video was complete, Abigail left the station. She drove home, cut her long hair, packed her suitcase and headed out of town. She knew she had to disappear from the world she had always known.

Abigail's disclaimer was on all the news stations, and the Carters and Porters breathed a big sigh of relief. Annie ran over to the Porters to hug Bob, who was so touched by the change of events he was in tears. That night everyone got together at the Carters and had a wonderful celebration. Barbara praised Bob and said, "Look what love and forgiveness did. Betty, maybe we should consider trying to love and forgive Madido."

Betty and Barbara looked at each other. Steve suggested, "Maybe if you visit Madido in prison and tell him we all forgive him, it will bring joy to us all."

Annie added with a smile, "Of course, women are much better at forgiveness than men."

Everyone laughed, and the evening ended with the kids playing a little Mozart and an arrangement of John Williams' "Star Wars" music.

CHAPTER

11

SISTERLY LOVE

Madido grew more and more depressed in his Perry State Prison cell. At this point in his life, at the age of nineteen, his happiness depended on being recognized as a terrorist and committed to die. But as the days went on and his isolation prevented him from hearing any news, he grew more and more morose. He began to realize that his happiness came when he knew he was appreciated, and he was now getting the message that he never would be.

Madido had grown up without ever being appreciated by his broken family. The propaganda that he had been exposed to through the internet and phone calls from the Middle East affected him. The recruiter who called him seemed so warm, and he assured Madido that the radicals' cause was good and he would be rewarded in heaven with seventy virgins. So when Mr. X contacted him, he felt appreciated by the radicals. He didn't realize it was actually the Mafia that was pushing him to shoot Bob, and not the radicals. Now he was cut off from all that, alone in prison and never going to be rewarded in heaven. He would spend the next sixty years in isolation. Then something happened that made him see a different heaven.

On June 16th Barbara and Betty, along with Bob and Annie, implored the prison warden to allow the two young giant women to spend some time visiting Madido. The warden said, "Why on earth should we allow them?"

Annie explained, "Perhaps we can find out who was behind the assassination attempt." The answer to that question was still a mystery.

A week later the prison warden called Bob to tell him that, after much discussion, it was decided that the young ladies could visit Madido. He suggested that they should take time to build a relationship and not inquire too soon as to who was behind the whole plot. This was just what Bob's team wanted.

The next day the prison guard entered Madido's cell and told him that two beautiful ladies were here to visit him. He was going to be allowed to come out to the prison garden and talk with them. "And by the way, these are the ladies that stopped you from shooting Bob Porter."

Madido was shocked. He didn't know what or how to think. When Betty and Barbara joined him in the garden, they towered over him. He kept his head low and didn't look up at them.

"Madido, we are here first to thank you for telling the

truth, which helped to get us released. That was very kind of you, and we appreciate it, and we appreciate you. That was very courageous. We and all our friends have you in our thoughts."

Madido couldn't believe what he was hearing. He had expected to be yelled at, degraded, ridiculed and criticized. Slowly he looked up at the beautiful giant ladies staring at him. It may have been the first time in his life that he felt truly appreciated. He began to have all kinds of thoughts. Maybe he should tell them the truth.

Then it happened. The love he felt in the garden moved him to tell the truth. He had never felt anything like this before. "Ladies, the truth is..."

Barbara interrupted, "Madido, when you confessed to your attempt to assassinate Bob, you were being moved by something greater than all of us to tell the truth. Look what this has meant to the world."

Madido was in heaven. His whole consciousness changed. His depression left him. "Maybe it was something greater than all of us that moved me."

Betty jumped in, "We've heard that you may have wanted to be given credit for trying to destroy someone who opposed the radical philosophy. But there is still something within you, greater than pride, that is now making you want to be truthful."

Madido was blown away. Here he was in prison for attempted murder, and his whole perspective on life was changed.

The girls were quiet. Seven foot tall Betty walked over to Madido and put her arms around him. "Madido, we care very much for you. You are so important to us. We'll be visiting you every week. Just let the guilt inside you blow away – like a mist."

Then the real shocker came as both ladies bent down and kissed Madido on each cheek. He couldn't believe what was happening. The guard came just then and led a joyful Madido back to his cell.

CHAPTER

12

FORGIVEN

It was a good thing that the Carters' living room was so spacious. The "family" was getting larger and larger. The Carters' new mansion up on the hill was, of course, much, much larger than all the other homes in the neighborhood. People would often ask why it was so much bigger than the ordinary sized homes all around them. When the Carters bought their beautiful "castle" years ago, they thought they would love the four hundred acres of lovely meadows spread out below them. But they missed having neighbors and decided to sell the acres and start a wonderful and unique housing development. Other families could live right next door, and become the neighbors they missed having.

And the Carters' home with its enormous living room was turning out to be an ideal place for the "family" to meet. Four kids were usually upstairs playing Monopoly or having a ping pong game in the basement. Bob and

Jane, along with Steve, Annie, Betty and Barbara, would enjoy delicious barbecues or great pot lucks, making the get-together evenings great fun.

"Oh, it was really a joy to meet with Madido," Betty told the "family". "He was the most sullen, depressed guy we've ever seen, and when we left he was smiling and actually returned our hugs. It was a magical experience for us!"

Steve asked with a little smile, "Maybe we should call you both the 'FF's for 'Friendly Females'."

Annie replied, "You all, this is turning out to be something really special. We seem to be working together and creating joy for each other. And this in spite of the fact that we have to deal with you little guys." Everyone doubled over with laughter.

"You know, Madido went from being a little monster to a nice man in only four minutes. I wish there was a way for him to start his life over. It was obvious that a little affection made a great impact on him. I guess he didn't get much love in his life. Barbara and I will visit him again. Thank you, Bob, for inspiring us."

Annie piped in, "You know, loving each other is probably what we should be doing more in our MWT meetings. I know so many of our women are deeply concerned about what has happened to them. And sharing their feelings has helped to ease the pain they feel. I know that being accepted by each other makes such a difference. And I know it broke the paralysis that depression caused me, which is why I joined MWT. Maybe we MWT women should focus more on finding ways we can help men who are suffering too. When men see that we can see them as who they really are, not just as big or small, handsome or... well, maybe not so handsome, they are uplifted. We certainly want to make men feel loved and not use our superior strength to intimidate them like some men did to us."

Steve added, "It sounds good to me. Annie, you know I always said you were beautiful in spite of the fact that your clothes were constantly busting on you every week, and you never said, 'Steve, just 'cause you're a skinny little guy I still love you'." Everyone was laughing.

Then Bob made another suggestion. "In keeping with our new approach to handling the effects of the sphere disaster, maybe we should try to find Abigail and invite her to be a part of our 'family' too."

Jane asked, "Where is she? I think she disappeared after she came out with the truth. She was probably afraid that whoever talked her into the scheme might punish her. How are we ever going to find her?"

Bob answered, "There's got to be a way. Any ideas?"

All of a sudden there was a knock on the Carters' front door. Steve opened it, and a tall lady stood there wrapped in a shawl. She said softly to Steve, "Do you know where your neighbors, the Porters, are? I need to thank Bob for his kindness and forgiveness."

Bob called from the living room, "I'm Bob, can I help you?"

The lady in the shawl asked if she could come in. Steve welcomed her, and she walked over to Bob. Taking off her scarf, she said, "I'm Abigail." There stood a bald lady.

The entire room was aghast. "My goodness, we were just talking about you. Are you dressed this way because you feel threatened?" Betty asked.

"I had to become someone else, or I knew I would not live so I had to disappear to stay alive."

"Abigail, you are welcome to stay in our home. We have a lot of extra bedrooms," Steve said.

Abigail sat down on the floor with her head bowed. She started to cry, and the room went very quiet. "God is having mercy on me. I was doing such an evil thing, but Bob forgave me, and now God must be forgiving me, too."

"But," Bob replied, "you're safe now and you are part of our 'family'. Your life will be with us. Welcome!"

CHAPTER
13

OH NO, NOT ANOTHER EVIL PLOT

Soapy was having a hard time facing what was happening to TG. Recruitments were down, some were leaving, but Bob's MWT was doing great. At their weekly staff meeting Rusty reported that TG's spies had been watching Bob at his home. But they were very sure he was often visiting his neighbors, the Carters, in their huge house up on the hill.

More importantly, the spies were convinced that a lot was happening at the mansion. There were many people living there. In fact, their assessment was that they were connected and contributing to the success of MWT. They were probably helping MWT plan a strategy to help the organization grow and have an impact on the nation. They had also seen several huge women who appeared to be living there.

Rusty joked, "Too bad there isn't a big tornado

heading for that mansion. That would solve our problems."

Soapy quietly said, "Tornados aren't the only powerful things in the world."

The staff was quiet. The meeting soon ended and everyone walked out without saying a word, but they looked at each other with very serious expressions on their faces.

Rusty made contact with Tony from the Mafia. "Are you aware of what's going on at the Carters' home?"

Tony responded, "Are you kidding? Of course we know. We will handle it soon."

At the next weekly TG meeting, Rusty passed on his conversation with Tony. Soapy was quiet again. Everyone looked at each other and was afraid to comment. It was obvious they all knew the Mafia was planning something. If they were to succeed, it certainly would benefit TG. But that would be a crime. Could they live with the guilt for not reporting their suspicions to the police? Trying to set up a false scene with Abigail at the post office was a crime, but this was an even deeper sin.

After a few minutes of silence, Soapy said, "I can't condone violence to solve our problem. Let's ponder this whole thing." But they all knew the longer they pondered the more likely all hell would break loose.

At the next Mafia meeting, Boss Giovanni began putting together the master plan to eliminate MWT. He lectured, "We know that the key members of the MWT movement are meeting several times a week at

Steve Carters' huge mansion at 2150 Sunset Street in Merrydale. We've been checking out the neighborhood, and one bomb can change the whole ball game. As before, we've found another radical nut who thinks our contact with him represents a religious terrorist group. Next Thursday he will knock on the door at 6:30, the time their group gets together and make believe he's delivering pizzas. When the door opens, he'll rush in and blow himself up, along with everyone in the room.

"We found out that 6:30 is when they have their ten minute meditation before supper. There should be fifteen people in the room. Our plot will destroy the entire leadership of MWT and more. It will scare prospective members who are thinking of joining. And it could be the end of MWT.

"It'll scare our wives, too. I know many of you have complained how they aren't taking orders like they used to. I heard about what happened to you, Charlie, when you smacked your wife for not bringing in the dessert right away after dinner. Apparently she hit you, which is why you have that black eye, right?"

"Yeah, but I'm not the only one being bullied by seven foot tall bitches."

Everyone yelled, "That's right, that's right!"

The meeting ended with everyone smacking each other's hand in high fives while yelling, "Hooray, hooray!"

That same night the "family" was getting together. After the meditation Steve announced he needed to talk about something he felt was very important. "With all the anger that TG is expressing towards Bob and Annie for all their good work, I'm led to believe that for our own safety we should be very alert. I know that the assassination attempt on you, Bob, and the trumped up infidelity scheme, have not been officially linked to the TG, but I'm suspicious that they were involved. In fact, the ideas were probably planted by them. If I'm correct, there is no question they will continue to try to destroy us, maybe in a very dramatic way."

Bob answered, "Steve, I've been thinking about this, too. I'm not sure what we should do differently, because I think we all love what we've been doing, and it sorta takes us out of our unique approach to life to bring in guards around our 'church'."

Annie said, "Oh Bob, I really understand your point of view, but I'm a mother and I don't want my kids to get hurt."

Bob replied, "Gotcha, Annie. Let's think about all this while we meditate."

The Mafia's plans were finalized, and Tony passed the bomb on to Randy, another radical convert who would be posing as a pizza delivery driver. Randy was going to make his fake pizza delivery to the mansion, and everything was in place. The mob had painted "Perfect Pizza" in huge letters on each side of the van. The bomb was so big it had to be placed in three pizza boxes that were converted into one big box.

***

The evening after the Mafia planned their horrible act, their wives had their own weekly get together. Little did their husbands know what was going on when the eight women met. They were actually putting together their own plan.

Margaret was the first to speak. "Well, girls, our efforts to find out what's going on at our silly husbands meetings has paid off. Francesca told me what our dumb little midgets are up to. The guys don't realize Fran has been listening to them while she brings them coffee and donuts. They think she doesn't understand Italian because she's a Mexican, but she does. At my suggestion she listened to their conversations at the door before she brought in the food. Also, she's tall enough to put her ears next to the heating vents, and she could hear what they were saying when she wasn't in the room. She's pretty sure she's got the whole picture."

Bella added, "I'm so glad we got her to join us on our project."

Margaret continued, "On Thursday night they are planning to kill everyone involved in leadership for MWT. They are sending some radical nut with a bomb to that mansion where Bob Porter meets with his allies."

"Oh no!" the ladies screamed. "What are we going to do?"

Margaret went on, "And I have come up with a plan, but we're going to need your help."

"Can't we just call the police?" Harriet asked.

"No," Margaret answered, "that would put our guys in jail, and then we wouldn't have the fun of ordering them around anymore, or bopping them on the head when they get out of line...like they used to do to us.

"Here is the plan. It's a little complicated because we're going to have to deal with some mob spies who will be watching for the bomb deliverer. Anyway, here's the plan."

CHAPTER

14

IT'S ABOUT TO HAPPEN

Thursday evening the Carters' mansion was bursting with music, joy and sixteen people. Bob glanced out the living room window and noticed the strangest thing. Bob laughed, "Look everyone! There are eight apparently Muslim really tall women parading back and forth in front of this place. They have signs that say Sign Up Now For The TGs. Are they serious?"

Steve asked, "Should we call the police?"

"No, but let's hold off our meditation until they leave."

Just then the mob's pizza van arrived. When Randy got out of the van and walked toward the mansion, two of the ladies grabbed him, took the pizza boxes away and shoved him back in the van. Two other ladies hopped in the van, closed the doors and drove off. The last four ladies walked up to the Carters' front door. Steve opened it before they rang the bell, since the "family" had been watching the whole scene, completely puzzled.

Steve stared at the ladies and asked, "What's going on here?" There was silence. One lady looked at her watch. More silence. Then there was the sound of a huge explosion in a large park a block away. The park was created by Steve and Annie when they set up their unique housing development.

One of the ladies said, "That bomb you just heard explode was going to be detonated in your living room. We warn you to guard yourselves." They turned around, ran and jumped into a taxi that had just arrived.

There followed a long meeting with the police at Steve's house that evening. No one had any idea who the Muslim women were or who the bomber was. The van had disappeared in the explosion. The "family" realized they were in danger and needed protection. Bob was not happy with the police orders for police to guard the mansion twenty-four hours a day.

But, believe it or not, the Neighborhood Association came up with an exciting plan that both Bob and Steve, and the police, agreed to. At the next Neighborhood Association meeting, Bob explained the plan. It was a plan that everyone liked.

"We all like to take walks in our own beautiful neighborhood that Steve and Annie created. So everyday let's have our big ladies and a couple small men circle the grounds. With all the ladies we've got here, each woman will only have to put in a couple of hours a week. And in spite of what that crazy Soapy doesn't want us to do, we can give them a gun or two.

No little guys are going to mess with our giants. This will show our support for MWT."

The press and TV coverage of these events helped spread the vision of MWT which was: "Let's value people for their spiritual qualities of courage, kindness and brother and sisterly love rather than their size, strength, race, gender or religion." This was not what TG and the Mafia were preaching.

Soapy was relieved that the latest assassination attempt, which he had kinda guessed was being planned, failed. He began to realize that his desire to make TG succeed was not as strong as the feelings of guilt he knew would encompass him if Bob had been killed, even if he had not been directly involved. This moved him to make a decision that was going to rock the nation.

CHAPTER
15

I'M GETTING
OUTTA HERE

Two days after the bomb plot failed, Soapy went on TV to announce that he was giving up the leadership of TG. His address ended with, "Violence is not the answer to the challenges our world faces. I still believe in some of the philosophy of TG but not all. And if TG inadvertently incites some people to consider violence as acceptable, I can no longer be a part of it." Later the president spoke to the nation commending Soapy's decision.

After the TV was turned off in the Carters' living room, Jane asked, "Would it be crazy to invite Soapy to join us some evening?"

Bob replied, "No, I think it's a good idea. We all learn something when we spend time with people who don't always agree with us. And his comments about violence are what the whole world needs to consider. I say, let's get him to join the 'family'."

But now the Mafia mob was in turmoil. The guys couldn't understand why their wives were smiling, and they never asked their husbands why they were so unhappy. They didn't seem to care about them.

"What happened to our great plot?" Giovanni asked.

One of the spies who witnessed the attempted bombing answered, "There were eight Muslim women dressed in black protesting outside the mansion with signs supporting TG. We left them alone 'cause they seemed to be on our side, but they were traitors. When Randy arrived with the bomb in the pizza box the Muslims grabbed him and the bomb, stole the van and drove off. Ten minutes later they blew up the bomb in a nearby park. The whole plan was a complete failure. Somebody must have known what was going to happen. There must be some spies in our mob."

Just then the door to the mob meeting room burst open and eight giant ladies rushed into the room. "Okay, you little jerks," Margaret declared, "You are going to listen to us. The mob is finished."

Giovanni asked, "Are you kidding? Get outta here."

One of the large wives, Suzanne, grabbed Giovanni by the seat of his pants and threw him against the wall. Then she turned him around and held him up close to the ceiling by his throat.

"Wait!" Giovanni's wife shouted. "That's my husband. Let me hold him up there." Then she took over.

"Okay men," Margaret continued, "here is the plan. The mob is finished. We are who stopped your horrible assassination attempt, and now we're going to give you the opportunity to change all our lives." The men were all silent as they peered up at the scary amazons.

"We've found something wonderful that you're going to do instead of beating people up, selling drugs and threatening everyone. We learned the local university needs a good Italian teacher. So, Benito, you will be hired by them next semester. And as for you, Henry, you're a complete computer whiz and have been doing all the stuff for the mob, so we found a small company that needs your skills. But the best new adventure for all of us is going to be something fantastic.

"This town has only one small lousy Italian restaurant. You all have been complaining about this for years. So, the rest of you are going to start a bigger and better Italian restaurant here in Merrydale. Most of you will cook while we help you get started."

Giovanni argued, "Are you nuts? You can't make us do that."

Eight ladies walked over to their husbands, threw them down on the floor and sat on them. This made them realize that there was not going to be any more discussion...it was a done deal.

Weeks later at one of their weekly "family" get-togethers, Bob mentioned, "Did you know we finally have a great Italian restaurant in town? And they deliver, too. Wouldn't it be terrific if we had some delicious pasta instead of our barbecued chicken every so often?"

Annie spoke up, "Yes, it's a terrific restaurant, and I'm sending an article to the paper about them."

Steve asked, "Have you also noticed the local paper reports that crime seems to have lessened? Wouldn't it be funny if the families running the restaurant were mafia guys who now have better jobs?"

Everyone laughed, and Jane said, "Come on now, don't be silly."

Soapy, who was attending the "family" gathering for the first time, really felt uncomfortable. He felt he couldn't tell everybody what he knew, or at least suspected, but something urged him to comment, "Nothing is impossible."

"Oh yes it is, Soapy. It's impossible for you to beat me at Scrabble," Bob joked.

And so the Scrabble games started. With so many people in the "family" now, they had to set up three boards. "Dessert and Scrabble with friends, what could be better?" Annie smiled.

Barbara and Betty went to see Madido every week, and he was always so happy that they came to spend time with him. After about six weeks of visiting Madido, Bob, Steve, Barbara and Betty went to the District Attorney to see if there was any possibility to get Madido out on bail if he would reveal who set him up to try to assassinate Bob. They told the D.A. that Madido seemed to have changed dramatically. His trial had not yet occurred, and there were all kinds of issues emerging. Was he sane at the time of the attempt? Was he sane now? Things were complicated, and both his defense lawyers and the prosecuting attorneys were laboring long and hard preparing for the upcoming trial.

The D.A. agreed that if Madido gave them information, he would consider releasing him in the custody of Steve Porter. Steve was a lawyer and was once a police officer and still had his credentials. Since Madido was only nineteen years old at the time of the incident, the D.A. felt compassion for him.

On the next visit to the jail, Bob and the ladies finally raised the crucial question. "Madido, were you ever encouraged to try to assassinate Bob?"

Madido answered, "Yes, I was approached by someone who claimed he was a terrorist. I had a lot of calls and emails from people in the Middle East, after I had subscribed to a radical website and became sympathetic to them. I was so depressed and felt no self-worth, and they started to give me purpose in life. Only now I can see what a horrible purpose it was.

"A young man who I met at Starbucks one day noticed how depressed I was. He sensed that I needed purpose. I didn't want to live, and so the idea of becoming a martyr for radical terrorists really hooked me. And having seventy virgins in heaven sounded pretty good too," he laughed.

"Who was the young man, Madido?"

"He told me his name was Ronald Barnes. After he gave me the gun, I never saw him again. Before I was imprisoned I went back to Starbucks many times with a scarf around my face, but I never saw him again."

Bob went to the D.A. with the latest information. Madido was secretly and quietly released to the custody of Steve Carter and lived in Steve's mansion. Madido was in heaven! He was invited to all the "family" gatherings, and his whole approach to life was transformed. But the "family" would soon witness another frightening event.

CHAPTER
16

AGAIN?
ARE YOU KIDDING?

While watching a "Downton Abbey" rerun Sunday night after supper, Bob, Jane, Steve, Annie, Barbara, Betty, Abigail and Madido heard a knock on Steve's front door. Steve opened it and there was their neighbor, Fred, staring at them. He had a puzzled look on his face halfway between a smile and a look of gloom.

"What's up?" Steve asked.

Fred responded, "The sphere is returning. The scientists say it might make women go back to their original size."

"Oh, come in," Jane said, "Tell us what you heard. We've been watching a DVD so we didn't see the news. That's unbelievable, just as unbelievable as what happened to us three years ago! What does everyone think?"

Annie spoke first. "Oh, I'm so happy that I might get to be who I really am again!"

"Not me," Jane laughed. "I love being stronger than Bob."

Steve joked, "Me neither. I loved having Annie open doors for me, and I hate to admit it, but I'm also into her long legs."

Bob finally added his feelings. "I think this whole experience has taught us so much. It's made us see each other differently. Instead of focusing on physical bodies, we've checked out our spiritual qualities. And if we didn't do that, we were in trouble...like I was when this whole thing first happened. I had to change the way I looked at the world, at others, as well as myself."

"Well, it really did shake up the world," Steve added. "Do you think when women go back to their 'normal' sizes, some of the good things people learned from the sphere's visit will stay with us?"

Jane said, "Some *have* learned and won't go back to their old ways of thinking. I've never said it before, but Bob was always great. And even though I loved him deeply, he always intimidated me. Now he doesn't. And I know with all my heart that Bob will treat me as he does now even when I do return to my smaller size. I think he's learned more than most of us from this experience."

Bob commented, "Yes, I did learn. But I believe the most important thing I learned was humility."

Annie jumped in, "That's funny. Humility wasn't the most important thing I had to learn."

Steve laughed, "That's true, Annie, you were always the most humble." He added softly, "And the most beautiful woman I'd ever met...other than Jane, Betty and Barbara."

Everyone laughed as Steve continued, "Your only problem was you never stuck up for yourself. I had to keep drawing you out. You didn't have to be pushy, just honest."

"I know, I know," Annie agreed, "but this whole mess got me thinking that women need to speak up more. I know it wasn't easy to do. Jane, can I tell what happened to us earlier in our lives?"

Jane sighed. "Yes."

"Jane was beaten by her first husband, and I was raped as a teenager. When I worked at a TV station as a correspondent, my boss threatened to fire me if I didn't have sex with him. So I was fired. Jane's husband only agreed to a divorce on the condition she didn't tell anyone about his abuse. And I didn't tell anyone what happened to me. But maybe we have to change this mind-set, though that's not easy. I felt so guilty and dirty after I was raped. I wanted so badly to forget it. Telling anyone seemed like it would make me feel even worse."

Jane agreed, "I know how you felt, Annie. I too, felt guilty that maybe I had done something so wrong that Ted was justified in hitting me. I guess I was kinda stupid. I just didn't want anyone to know what was going on in our home."

Annie butted in, "I know this is a shock to all of you. But if all women who were physically abused or sexually assaulted had reported the crime, I bet a lot of men, might have thought twice before they did something like that.

Steve, you never pushed me around. You were always gentle and kind, a real man. But while working with our MWT I saw many women who had been treated badly by men, often their husbands or coworkers or bosses. So when women became the bigger people physically, men were encouraged to communicate, rather than push us down as some did when we were smaller."

Bob and Steve were dumbfounded!

"Annie, I never knew this happened."

Then Bob cried out, "Oh, Lord help us. Jane, why didn't you ever tell me about all this?"

"Because Bob, we needed to move forward and put this behind us. We must not keep bringing it up."

Annie added, "Of course we should have reported what happened immediately, as everyone else should do today, but as Jane said, we must now move forward and put these things behind us...we must feel now that these horrors never happened to us and know that our purity has never been taken from us."

Jane finished with, "Also, in the future the wonderful women movements starting and growing all over the country should be great support groups for women everywhere. When women report crimes done to them, like ones done to Annie and me, they won't be alone anymore. I believe I heard that a famous senator once indicated that soon women will have collective power because of the women's movements. With other women with them, they will be able to speak out with less fear."

After Jane's last comments there seemed to be a great

peace and calm felt by all. Everyone in the room had been respectfully quiet during all the serious revelations.

After some moments of silence Bob said, "Well this 'family' get-together certainly has been special." After more quiet Bob, thinking that it might be wise to move on, said, "I wonder how the rest of you feel about the return of the sphere and what the future might have in store for us."

Madido spoke up first. "I don't know what to think about the future, but I certainly am grateful for the sphere's first visit. This experience changed my life. Barbara and Betty, you were the key players in the show. I'm actually joyful now, and I had been so depressed before."

He continued, "If I had not met you, Mr. Carter, I would have never had any interest in the law. By letting me assist you in your office, you got me interested in going back to school if I ever get out of this mess. And the 'family's' willingness to contribute to my tuition — well, what can I say? I'm so glad that sphere came and that I've changed. I can deal with my life now."

Barbara and Betty smiled, and it was obvious they were delighted by what Madido had said.

The kids had been playing music upstairs, and when they stopped and came down to hear the news, they were absolutely gleeful.

There were many questions. When was it coming back? Would it really return women to their former sizes? What was in the future for everyone? Would all hell break loose again?

The news about the predicted return of the sphere shook the planet. The clothing industry would boom again because sales would skyrocket. Barbie dolls might reappear in the toy stores. The Lakers, on the other hand, were dismayed because Rachel Good, their eight foot tall superstar, might shrink. The women's team owners were delighted of course. Their stars might be coming back.

Some Middle Eastern men were ecstatic and thought they would be able to order their wives around again. But they kept it to themselves. Many ladies were sad they wouldn't have beautiful gigantic legs to show off, and the men felt just the same. But they kept quiet.

The big question was still, when would it happen? It was very strange, because the scientists couldn't predict an exact date. Their best guess was two or three months. That remained to be seen.

The next morning at Folcano's Restaurant, the mobsters and their wives had breakfast before planning the rest of the day. The guys were laughing and excited that they again might be taller than their wives. The wives, however, had mixed feelings about the predictions for their future. One guy shouted, "We can go back to being real mobsters again."

While the men all laughed, the ladies scowled down on them. "Look you dummies, we aren't there yet, and if you aren't careful we'll grab you and lock you up." More laughter.

Giovanni jumped in, "Listen everybody. Bob Porter and his 'family' made reservations for next Tuesday night. This will make us famous. Forget the mob stuff. This is much better than our old world."

They all stood and jubilantly raised their glasses of orange juice in a toast to the future. "And ladies, I'm gonna promise that we'll work together as equals, even when you go back to being midgets, 'cause you were the ones who came up with the great restaurant idea. It's so much more fun than selling drugs. We owe it to you. And we're not using the 'F' word anymore."

Everybody was happy and started exchanging hugs, and they just couldn't wait for Tuesday to come when a panel of some of the world's most prominent scientists would debate on TV the return of the sphere.

Unfortunately the news was a bit unsettling. Practically the whole country was glued to the TV for the debate and what possible effects it would have on the earth's inhabitants. Were the women going to grow even taller, or were they going to go back to their original size? The scientists were at least able to agree that the sphere would be back in approximately two months.

The next day all hell broke loose around the country. Sports teams weren't sure what to do. So many had hired huge women and wondered how they could get out of their contracts if the new teammates went back to being smaller. Or what if they grew even larger? The women were upset because they had no idea what would happen to them. Of course the men didn't know what to expect either. Realizing the turmoil sweeping the nation, the president made a brilliant decision and invited Bob and Annie to address the nation.

"My fellow Americans, it is with deep gratitude that I introduce to you Bob Porter and Annie Carter, who have graciously agreed to offer some of their insights regarding the challenging times we face. We have endured three years of one of the greatest challenges in our history, and I am so proud of this nation. During that time you have strived valiantly to comfort one another, even in the midst of your own fears.

"In spite of the turmoil created by the sphere that circled our world, we have seen incredible improvements in many areas of our nation. Domestic abuse statistics have declined dramatically. Equal pay for equal work among women is becoming the norm. Sexual harassment of all kinds is declining, and in fact has practically ceased.

"There have been numerous social improvements in many countries around the world. Forced marriages for eleven year old girls, many close to seven feet tall, has dwindled to almost none. Women's rights have increased dramatically. In short, we are making it through this crisis.

"The secret to our survival has been compassion and love for each other. Now, with the unknown effects coming soon with the sphere's reappearance, we must join together and have confidence that we can face whatever challenges are presented. And now, Bob and Annie, will you be so kind as to help us prepare for whatever the future may bring?"

Bob let Annie step up to the podium first. "Women, even if we go back to our former selves, we will have grown in our understanding of life and in the way we should really view ourselves and others. Let's look at ourselves as wonderful creations of the good Lord, both men and women, with qualities of tenderness, warmth, goodness and kindness, and not just as physical beings. Actually we all have feminine and masculine qualities, and that makes us one. If we must grow taller still, we can handle it just as we have handled what we have already endured. If we go back to our original sizes, many of us will be very grateful and will appreciate all we have learned from this experience. And heaven help us if we do get bigger, let's continue to refrain from taking revenge on some men who mistreated us when we were smaller than them. Continue to forgive, and trust men will be touched by our understanding."

Annie continued, "I once learned a prayer, I think it was the Prayer of St. Francis, that began 'Lord, make me an instrument of thy peace; where there is hatred let me sow love, where there is injury, pardon...' Maybe we should all remember those words."

Bob then added, "Annie has made some wonderful points. We men have also learned much from this experience. I think we are more aware of what women have had to endure now that we've walked in their shoes for a while. Because of the sphere, men have had similar experiences and can see who we really are. We must be comforting, respectful and supportive to the wonderful women in our lives. So many of us have learned to appreciate how women protect us, not the other way around. The bottom line, I think, is we have learned to view each other more spiritually than physically from this strange experience."

The president ended his remarks with, "Americans, let us comfort and support each other during the next months as we await the return of the sphere. When it arrives, know that no matter how it affects us, it cannot break us apart. We are one, man and woman, woman and man. The value of human life knows no gender. This is true for intellectual, as well as physical and spiritual, abilities of men and women.

"I would like to finish with an excerpt from a speech given by Michelle Obama to a group called Let Girls Learn, concerning intellectual equality for women. She said: 'The more I traveled and met with girls and learned from experts...the more I realized that the barriers to girls' education aren't just resources. It's not just about access to scholarships or transportation or school bathrooms. It's also about attitudes and beliefs—that girls simply aren't worthy of an education; that women should have no role outside the home; that their bodies aren't their own...'

"In addition, UN studies have shown that allowing girls to get an education in countries such as Pakistan is a plus for the world's economy. It will increase and be key to ensuring global prosperity. I believe this is a very important aspect of our goal to promote peace between men and women at this historic time."

But the question that remained on everyone's mind was still, "What is the sphere going to do to us this time?"

At the weekly "family" gathering Abigail, along with all the others, congratulated Annie and Bob for their inspiring messages. "I'm so grateful that we have our 'family' here. Annie and Steve, we really appreciate your kindness inviting all of us to your lovely home. And now, as 'family', let us lock arms together and know that no matter what the future brings, we will survive. "Bob, you have taught us so much. You've taught us that each one of us can really change for the better."

"Thanks for your kind words, Abigail. Actually, so many of us have gone through change, both in our thinking and in our sizes. Our changes have made all of us better people. So let's know that whatever the sphere showers on us, it will be an opportunity for us to grow more…to make even more progress. We're stronger than any sphere."

"Yeah," the "family" members shouted together.

The wonderful peace the "family" enjoyed was not typical in the rest of the country, or the world for that matter. Many men worried matters would get even worse for them. And some women were afraid forced or arranged marriages would start again if they shrunk back to normal. Those women had enjoyed being able to call the shots for the last three years. So while they were still able to speak up, they tried to get the message out, "Hey, let's change things permanently no matter what happens."

Sports teams were held in limbo. The clothing industry was one entity that wasn't worried, no matter how things went. Either way, taller or shorter people were going to need new clothes. And the suppliers were going to make a fortune.

In the Middle East there had been horrendous turmoil for the past three years as many women claimed a better place in society. The men were fearful the returning sphere could possibly make women even larger! But on the other hand, they thought if it made women shrink back to normal size, it would really be great.

Since no one knew what to expect, negotiations were in process all over the world. The men and women were both offered to make deals. Lawyers were busier than ever before in history. If nothing else happened, at least most men recognized women's strength...their spiritual strength and the strength of their wisdom. "What if" was the beginning of all negotiations. Much of the communication would not have happened at all if everybody knew what was going to occur in two months. But the sphere knew, and she was going to surprise everyone.

CHAPTER

17

NOW THEY HAVE
A REAL CHALLENGE

Two months of uncertainty passed, the entire world was on pins and needles, as the sphere's arrival was expected soon. Most people didn't want anything to happen. Both men and women worried that the women would grow taller. Even though the women's height advantage had caused men to be nicer to them, women didn't want to grow any bigger.

All the "family" members prayed day and night to understand that the good Lord was in control of the situation. Bob assured everyone at the regular "family" get-together that everything would be all right. "Look how far we've come in the last three years. So many of us were on different sides of the river, and just look how we've come together. That wonderful quote from the Bible, '...all things work together for good to them that love God...' sure has been true for us. No matter what happens, we'll stick together and help others deal with the situation regardless how it turns out. Hey, let's take a look at the latest news!"

In order to get the very latest word, TV news shows reported the last minute deals negotiated all over the world. And then it happened.

The sphere arrived in the middle of the night above the U.S. and it circled the globe four times. Next morning the entire world silently watched TV. After the sphere left, people started asking each other, "Do you feel anything?" Everyone was again in a state of high anxiety as the scientists tried to determine how the vibrations cascading down to earth were going to affect the planet's populace.

After a week of nervous waiting, men the world over began to notice changes happening to some, but not all of them. Some men grew taller, a situation as puzzling as what occurred when the sphere visited three years earlier. Why weren't all men getting taller like the women did in the earlier event?

Scientists and doctors examined a large sample of men, both those who grew taller and those who didn't, to see what the difference was between those affected by the rays and those not. But after a month of research no one was able to come up with an explanation for this strange phenomenon. The word on everyone's lips was "Why?"

At the next "family" meeting, everyone gathered after supper in the grand living room. They watched a TV talk show with a discussion among men who had not grown taller and men who had. About a half-hour into the program Bob made a comment, "Has anyone noticed anything different between the tall men and the 'normal' ones? And why are all the men in our 'family' growing taller?"

Steve responded, "No, I didn't notice anything except that maybe the taller ones seem a little more soft spoken. Maybe their growth has affected their vocal cords?"

Abigail suggested, "Maybe the bigger men are more humble."

Betty added, "Well, at least they don't scare me anymore, even if they are bigger."

Madido said, "The big men seem kinda nice. I wish my dad had been more like them."

Bob smiled as he said, "I think you all have hit the nail on the head. It appears to me that there's a huge psychological difference between the men not affected by the rays and those who were, no matter what their original size. It's possible that those growing taller have quieted down because they're troubled by their new size, but I'm not sure."

Bob asked Steve, Madido and Soapy, "Does the fact that you are growing so much taller trouble you?"

"No," they all answered.

"Well, I'm going to call CNN and ask them to have a psychologist interview a hundred men, fifty big and fifty normal. I have a suspicion that the men's mental attitudes may have something to do with this phenomenon."

A few weeks later the "family" gathered again to watch

the news. The broadcast revealed results of the study which determined rays from the sphere only affected men who had a sense of humility and that mental state relaxed their genes, so the rays were free to make them grow. Incredibly, two men from the group of smaller men who apologized to the psychologist for their rudeness, started to grow three days later. This actually shocked them. Their apology wasn't offered because they wanted to grow, but because they were sincerely sorry, ashamed and embarrassed that they let their frustration get the best of them. The first stage of humility had occurred. The experts determined that humility, which fosters love, was the only way the rays could affect men's chromosomes, making them taller than women just as they had been before. Relative heights were now similar as they were prior to the sphere's first appearance. There was yet more shocking news for the world.

As some men grew taller, those who didn't were not happy. Six months after the sphere's return, the relative size of women to men, who expressed humility, kindness and warmth, was just as it had been before the sphere's initial appearance. But many people were now larger than their previous size before the sphere's first visit.

Once again, the garment industry rejoiced. They could hardly keep up with the demand for new clothes!

On the other hand, men's sports teams were in a state of complete confusion. "Do we keep these gals or not?"

Carpenters were delighted because they had so

many jobs enlarging doors and adding stairs, while the furniture industry was working around the clock manufacturing bigger beds and tables. Terrorist groups were in a real quandary, because their male fighters did not develop humility. And without humility, they remained intimidated because of their small size.

Men who hadn't changed from their original size before the first sphere visit were furious and wrestled with their dilemma. Why didn't this humility thing happen to the women? Many tall women had absolutely no humility, were pushy and complete egotists...they should never have grown taller. What was the answer to that? As it turned out, the answer to that question was just around the corner.

A year passed without another return of the sphere circling the earth, and changes gradually occurred on every continent. It was a slow process, but many men and women began to talk to one another with more respect that anyone had thought possible. More and more men were losing their urge to be bossy. And arrogance was definitely not tolerated.

Women now had to deal with something else as well— the need for humility now. It was apparently the correct order of things. First the sphere enlarged all women, because they already had humility from being treated as inferiors by men all the way back to the caveman. This gave them no choice but to be humble. But now they required a deeper humility in order to maintain their bigger size.

Perhaps this was the best way for women to learn

lessons. First men had to deal with their character, now it was time for women to learn a little more humility. Some women were furious, because those who had been aggressive and arrogant began to shrink. Others thought it was ridiculous, claiming that they were humble enough already. Apparently the sphere's rays didn't agree with them.

The latest phenomenon began to affect the dating game. Tall men and women knew a big date was a sure bet. At first small men, and now again small women, who didn't want to give up their big egos complained, "Look, I'm great, and that guy thinks he's great, too. So why can't we have a good time bossing each other around?"

Marriage was a little more complicated. When a little husband yelled and bullied his seven foot tall wife, she just tenderly picked him up and locked him in the bathroom like a child. "When you feel like calming down, little one, I'll be happy to let you out."

When a giant humble husband was cruelly berated by his tiny wife, he would smile and remain quiet. He certainly didn't want to start shrinking!

But the world began to realize humility wasn't something you could just turn on and off. It had to be real, and it wasn't that easy to attain. Therapists, preachers, psychologists and counselors made fortunes. Their clients wanted to grow physically, but not necessarily spiritually, so hypocrisy wasn't working for them. Hypocrites didn't grow physically or spiritually. Authors published many books dealing with humility, and the book stores couldn't keep up with the demand.

Many people didn't know what humility was, or how to get it. However, scientific evidence proved that whatever it was, it was helping people to grow stronger. The message spread more and more effectively. People began to realize that if they were humble, they could maintain their oversized bodies, or grow from their small size to join the "big boys and girls". They would then return to their previous relative sizes, just as they were before the first sphere. But if they didn't have true humility, the growth rays from the sphere had no effect on them.

All the small men and shrinking women were desperate to understand what humility was and how they could get it. "We need it. We want it," they all cried. "We want to stand tall and be up there with everyone else."

And then it happened. Scientists finally discovered the secret to getting humility.

CHAPTER
18

THE SECRET IS OUT

Everyone was so excited at the weekly "family" gathering. A special TV broadcast was scheduled that evening, and they planned to watch it. After dinner they took their places on the big sofas and chairs surrounding the huge TV screen and settled in to enjoy being together. Everyone got quiet.

The president came on stage, followed by professors and acclaimed psychologists from leading universities. They were joined by religious leaders from every denomination.

"Fellow Americans and citizens of the world," the president began, "we are here tonight to tell you what may be one of the most important scientific discoveries of all time. As we all know, our world has had two most unusual encounters with a strange sphere in the past four years which has affected mankind in a variety of ways. Although these encounters have presented many challenges, we have also learned much from them.

"Before we share the latest discovery made by these esteemed scientists, psychologists and religious leaders, I will remind you all of the most important information that was discovered last year. Researchers discovered that humility was the only human quality needed to enable the sphere's rays to affect one's growth. Humility was the one quality necessary to take advantage of the strange vibrations and to prevent a reversal of growth.

"But how do we attain humility? That was the one question we were all asking, and we believe we finally have the answer."

The president paused and turned to the dignitaries standing behind him on the stage. With one voice the entire group softly said two words, "Unselfish Love." They repeated those two words over and over with great reverence, as a choir might chant a familiar hymn. The effect on the audience was magical. People worldwide sighed and smiled, as did Bob and the "family".

The president turned back to the camera and spoke again. "Isn't this incredible? If we want to gain humility we must love others as ourselves. Even put others before ourselves and if we do that, we'll grow in so many ways. We will grow spiritually, and physically we will grow to the normal relative sizes we were before the sphere's visit." Bob and the "family" applauded loudly along with the audience.

The president continued, "And if you are already at the standard size, you won't shrink." More applause.

"Remember what the Bible says in 1 Corinthians, 'Now abideth faith, hope, love, these three; but the greatest of these is love'."

"So, if we love our neighbor, our boss, our mate and even those who aren't so easy to love, our physical size will either stay put or it will return to what is our normal relative size to all those who have gained true humility. If we find ourselves shrinking all we have to do is love everyone. And as I said before, love will make us grow in so many ways.

"Just think. If everyone put others before themselves, then everyone would have humility and love would take over, wars would cease, crime would disappear, injustice would evaporate and lawyers would have to find another profession! It would be a much better life to live on this earth. We all need to know that all good is possible."

When the president finished, one religious leader stepped forward to end the broadcast. "All of us standing here tonight agree that unselfish love is the core of all our religions. These sphere visits have made us examine ourselves. So on behalf of my colleagues, to all of you listening tonight, know that you can be the salt of the earth. Love others so you can develop humility and become the exact perfect size, and you will inspire others. As James said, 'Humble yourselves in the sight of the Lord and He shall lift you up'. When we love God first and have the humility to recognize the Lord as supreme, totally good and loving us unconditionally, we find that we will be loving others more."

With that the broadcast ended, with everyone shaking hands and hugging each other. Viewers all over the country went to bed that night pondering what they had heard. Would the world get the message?

What the world so recently learned actually began to sink in, if very slowly. At their next "family" gathering, Bob suggested that rather than watching TV after dinner, they get together in Annie and Steve's living room to talk about love. Everyone agreed and was enthusiastic about discussing the concept.

Steve started the discussion with a really positive declaration. "Well, whatever love is, we all seem to be expressing it. Everyone in this room seems to be the proper size relative to what we were before the sphere's visit. So I guess we are all fairly humble, and we certainly seem to express it by loving each other. But not all men and women around the world have figured it out yet."

Abigail spoke up, "Bob, you certainly expressed love when you forgave me for my stupid act."

Bob replied, "And I thank you, Abigail. I think you expressed even more love and humility by confessing you were a part of that deceptive scheme."

Soapy jumped in, "I guess humility is also accepting that you might have done something wrong. Confess it and then, most importantly, don't repeat that mistake."

Barbara said enthusiastically, "So just what is love? Hey, let's play a game. Everyone gets a point for coming up with one quality of love, okay? Who wants to keep score?"

Madido shouted, "I will!"

The words, "tenderness," "respect," "honor," "comfort," "unselfishness," and many others were shouted all at once.

"Hey, wait a minute. I can't keep score if you all shout at once," Madido smiled. And so they worked out a plan, and Annie eventually won with the most words.

There was no question the world was affected by all the information spread across the continents. Nations communicated with each other in much friendlier ways. Tensions eased and some wars even ended. Divorces in the U.S. declined from 60% to 8%. Political campaigns were far more civil. Drug use decreased as happiness and pleasure came from the "high" of friendship, rather than chemical substances. Robberies decreased and religious radicalism slowly tapered off. Prejudice faded.

Things looked good. More and more people smiled at each other, and the few remaining proportionately shorter women or men were greeted with hugs and smiles. Soon, they started to smile back at people, and they began to grow back to the new normal proportions. The clothing industry was still the best investment.

Then it happened. The next stage of the lesson from the sphere presented itself.

CHAPTER

19

WHEN ON EARTH IS THIS GOING TO STOP?

A year later, after so much progress was made all over the world, it happened. It was on every news channel and in all the papers. Another sphere raced toward the earth. People were shocked, and cried, "Oh no! Help us, good Lord!" in every language around the world. Everyone questioned, "After all the progress we have made, why another visit from the sphere?"

Many religious leaders told their congregations not to worry and to remember the verse from 1 Corinthians: "By the grace of God I am what I am: and his grace which was bestowed upon me was not in vain."

"This experience will not make any important change in our lives," clergymen told the people. "We've learned so much from these spheres. How to have humility. How to love. How to end war. Perhaps the good Lord is sending us a new experience to teach us even more."

Scientists and psychologists, however, were not going down that path. They wouldn't believe anything that couldn't be supported by physical evidence.

Bob asked the "family" to sit together and just be quiet and pray. They started by holding hands, then sat back and were still. Soapy made only one comment. "Family," he said, "this fits perfectly with that quote from the Bible, 'Be still and know that I am God'." They all remained still for an hour.

Then they hugged each other, got out their Scrabble boards and quietly played their favorite game. They didn't stay up late, because the sphere was predicted to arrive early, and they wanted to be awake when it appeared. But before going to bed, they took a moment to admire the beautiful full moon shining in a clear blue sky.

The next day the world was quiet. Everyone looked toward the skies in silent anticipation of what was to come. Whether it was 3 a.m. or 2 a.m. or 7 p.m., it didn't matter. Wherever people were on earth it was their duty to watch and pray. Finally it came.

Just as before, the sphere circled the earth twice. All military personnel put their weapons down. All sport events stopped. Boxing matches ceased. Mary Bund, that giant woman boxer, dropped her arms, and the much smaller guy she was fighting gratefully did the same. Amazingly, her opponent then started to grow.

After the sphere left, the whole world remained quiet. Everyone looked at each other to see if anything was happening. They did this even though scientists predicted it would probably take a week for any changes to take effect.

True to those predictions, one week after the sphere's spin around the earth it began to happen. At first it wasn't clear exactly what effects the sphere's visit had produced. People's bodies were growing in many different directions. But the bottom line was that everyone was returning to their original size. Some naturally tall women were still not as tall as they had been recently, but their size was now what it had always been before the first sphere. Soon everyone sensed what was happening.

Little by little, civilization began to rejoice over its new condition. Sure, it had been fun for many women to be so tall that they could dominate their husbands, but they really preferred their previous size and just hoped their husbands had learned something from being in their shoes for the last few years. And yes, many women had learned things as well.

Then yet another extraordinary event shook the world.

CHAPTER
20

A WAKE-UP CALL

Bob woke up early. He had had the strangest dream, and he wanted to tell Jane about it. Normally he would have pushed her a little to wake her up, but something was telling him to be quiet. He thought to himself, *Of course that was just a dream, but it's sure making me do some serious thinking.*

An hour later, Jane yawned as she slowly woke up, but suddenly she was wide awake. "Bob, where are you?"

"I'm in the kitchen fixing breakfast."

"What? I don't get it You always woke me up to fix your breakfast, and now you're fixing me breakfast? What's come over you?" She stood in the kitchen watching him.

Bob replied, "I'm not sure, but I had the strangest dream last night."

"You did?" Jane responded. "So did I. This is really weird. In my dream you were a completely changed man."

Bob laughed, "I changed in my dream too, and you also grew two feet taller."

Jane's jaw dropped. They both were silent.

Finally Jane said, "Wait a minute. That happened in my dream too! Come on, this is crazy. Did we leave the TV on or something before we went to sleep? What show were we watching last night?"

Bob answered, "We watched the Lakers' game."

"Oh, that's right. But, Bob, you won't believe this. In my dream a woman named Rachel Good was the eight foot tall star of the Lakers."

That did it. Bob dropped the pan with the scrambled eggs, and they both plopped down in their kitchen table chairs.

Annie and Steve were eating breakfast, too. Steve laughed, "Annie, I had the funniest dream last night. You won't believe it but..."

Annie interrupted him laughing, "I bet my dream was funnier than yours. This crazy sphere came over the earth and..."

"Wait, wait, don't tell me," Steve butted in. "That's what happened in my dream, too. Wait a second. Turn on the news."

They ran over to the TV and turned on CNN. They watched expectantly for ten minutes, but there was no news about a sphere circling the earth. They turned the TV off, and there was a knock on the door. Jane and Bob stood there with puzzled looks on their faces.

"Annie and Steve, can we talk for a minute?"

"Sure, Bob. What's up?"

The Porters walked quietly into the living room and sat down. "We were wondering if we should see a psychologist, because something really strange happened to both of us last night."

As they told what they had experienced, Steve and Annie were flabbergasted. Annie spoke first, "Wait, wait, don't tell us any more. Steve and I had that same dream."

What did this all mean?

What was going to happen next? A lot. This was only the beginning.

Giovanni, the Mafia leader, was very confused because of the dream he just had. He quickly got out of bed, ran to his car and drove to the nearest Catholic church to see a priest.

"Father, I need to confess. I had a strange dream last night."

The priest listened for a few minutes and then said, "Giovanni, I'm hearing this: 'Peace be still, and know that I am God.' I've had to work with that wonderful verse because..." he paused, "I had that same dream."

Giovanni answered, "Something is happening here, Father. Do you know that I'm the Mafia capo here in town?"

"I just learned that in the dream," answered the priest. "But apparently you quit doing that, and then you opened a great Italian restaurant."

"Not yet, Father."

Giovanni returned home and called a meeting of his men. They came into his office with perplexed looks on their faces, and Giovanni asked, "Did anyone have a strange dream last night?"

Everyone in the room answered, "Yeah."

He went on, "As your boss I'm gonna tell you we are gonna start operating differently than what we've been doin' up to now. No more shooting, no more threatening, no more offensive language. We're gonna open the best Italian restaurant in town." The group cheered.

There was a knock on the door, and Tony opened it. It was their wives. "Boys," Margaret said, "it may be hard to believe, but we girls all had a dream last night, and we wanna tell ya about it. It occurred to us that maybe the good Lord was telling us something. So we want you to listen to us, because what we're going to tell you guys to do could change all our lives."

"Hey, you girls aren't gonna have to tell us anything," Giovanni snapped back. "We guys also had the same dream, and we're gonna follow our dreams, not yours."

"But can't we at least tell you what our dreams were first?"

"Well, that's probably okay. One of the things we heard in our dream was it ain't a big deal to be the first one to speak, so go ahead."

The women were all startled by that. Margie said, "This is incredible! We must have all had the same dream, because in our dreams you guys actually listened to us. Anyway, we were told in the dream to forget the 'business', and instead start a legitimate Italian restaurant."

That did it. It was one of the first times that sixteen Italians in one room were all silent.

***

When Madido woke up in his shabby one-room apartment, he thought something had happened to him during the night that might be about to change his life. He had had the most wonderful dream and, at least for the moment, it seemed to have lifted the dark cloud of depression that had surrounded him for years. He thought, *I wonder if those wonderful people in my dream actually do exist. Is there a Barbara and a Betty? And a Bob? I think his name was Robert Porter.*

He looked up the name "Robert Porter" in the phone book. There were two Robert Porters, and he spent the whole morning wondering whether or not he should try contacting Bob. Finally he called the first of the two that were listed. A man answered, and Madido spoke nervously into his cell phone, "Mr. Porter, my name is Madido. Does that name ring a bell with you?"

It was the right Robert Porter, and Bob was blown away when Madido identified himself. "Madido," he asked, "did you have a dream last night about me?"

"Yes," Madido answered.

Bob quickly asked for his cell number, "We are going to have to get together."

Betty and Barbara met for breakfast and couldn't

wait to tell each other about the strange dreams they each had last night. But just like it was happening all over the world, when one person started telling a friend or spouse or daughter, or whomever about their dream, they could hardly get a word in edgewise before the other one said, "Hey, that was what I dreamed, too!"

It seemed like everyone on earth had the same dream. Even those who were fighting wars or taking drugs, and committing robberies or other crimes. The world had been jolted by the dream the night before and perhaps the dream told humanity to stop all selfishness and realize we all have one collective consciousness, for we are all one.

Soapy, a CEO, tried to make contact with Bob Porter. Abigail, who worked for a veterinarian, thought her dream was pretty unusual. She also searched for Bob and Jane, hoping to make contact.

The next time the Porters and the Carters were together, they watched the news before playing Scrabble. It was broadcast worldwide that there was a strange phenomenon occurring around the globe. It seemed unbelievable, but research showed people on every continent had the same dream about a sphere's visit to earth. Of course each person had their own personal experience in their dream, but many common factors were experienced by all. A sphere visited the earth in everyone's dream, and its effects on human bodies were the same. The characters in their dreams were people they knew. Also, the words truth, humility, grace, kindness, respect and love appeared in all their dreams and in their own language.

The commentators said people the world over were filled with euphoric joy after experiencing "The Dream."

This wonderful phenomenon made the world pause. It seemed all conflict stopped.

CHAPTER
21

A REAL FAMILY

While the Porters were enjoying dinner, Steve came up with a suggestion, "Wouldn't it be wonderful to create the 'family' we all had in our dream?"

Bob said, "Yes. And believe it or not a guy by the name of Madido called me. And remember Barbara and Betty? They called, too. I guess they're calling me because the dream maker made me the hero in the story. And, oh my gosh, remember that character, Soapy? He also called. I've got all their numbers. Let's all get together next week and celebrate. Would that be all right with you, Steve and Annie?"

"Absolutely."

Bob had another idea. "Oh, by the way, I wonder if we could include one more couple?"

"Who?" Annie asked.

"Well, they were in our dreams too. Remember Giovanni and his wife, Margaret?"

"Oh yes," Annie replied. "But they were Mafia thugs, and I don't think we would want them here."

Bob answered, "They're not Mafia thugs anymore. They're starting a legitimate business, an Italian restaurant."

"Okay, yes, yes, let them come!" What a wonderful end to the dream. As the Porters left, the Carters yelled with a laugh, "Sweet dreams."

The next "family" get-together was a spectacular pot luck event with close to twenty people who had become acquainted in "The Dream." Everyone hugged, and they laughed and cried all at once. They enjoyed wonderful salads, delicious chicken and incredible pasta.

After the meal, the kids played some quartets, and Giovanni, who had brought his violin, played some Country Western music. Bob said, "Giovanni, how on earth did you learn Country Western music coming from an Italian family."

"Well, as a kid I had to play a lot of Vivaldi, but I got hooked listening to Country Western music when I first heard it on the radio. At first I played it secretly, but then I just went back and forth between Vivaldi and Country. Wanna hear what I did?" Everyone enthusiastically begged him to demonstrate what he had done as a kid.

It turned out to be a memorable evening, and near the end Bob stepped forward and said, "Well, everybody, we're a great gang here. We're all people who listened. It may have taken some jolts in our lives to wake us up, I know it did with me, but we have changed. If I hadn't experienced 'The Dream' last month I might still be bossing Jane around." Everyone had a good laugh.

"Oh, Bob, it was so much fun to be two feet taller than you and push you around." More laughter, more hugging and more promises for all to get together every week and enjoy "family" togetherness.

As everyone got ready to go home, there was a loud banging on the door. Steve opened it and found his neighbor, Fred, standing there with a panicked look on his face.

"Steve, there was a warning on the TV news just a few minutes ago. Apparently there's some strange sphere circling the earth and sending out terrible vibrations that are really dangerous. Everyone should be quiet and take shelter in their basements."

Steve laughed. "Oh my goodness, Fred, are you trying to fool us? Don't you know about 'The Dream'?"

Fred smiled and said, "I do, but you all seem to be having so much fun, I wanted to join the party. So I had to think of some way to 'crash the party,' and make you laugh.

"And I bet you're all thinking what I'm thinking. That maybe the good Lord let us experience 'The Dream' in order to teach us how we ought to treat one another. To love and respect one another, no matter what our differences of opinion are, or our gender, size, physical strength, religion, nationality, color or lack thereof. We must love unselfishly. Isn't that what you all are thinking?" Everyone grabbed each other's hands, formed a circle and cheered their approval.

Then Steve suggested, "Hey, maybe what we think is real is only a dream. Is life really just a dream?"

Annie quietly answered, "Actually I feel that eternal life and love are God's gifts to us all and if we look up in our thought we will see the truth."

Still holding hands the "family" softly added, "And in this true, eternal life we must love, love, love."

And guess what? The women's movements throughout the world continued to grow, and women rising embraced the world in their love.

Any comments regarding "Women Rising" can be sent to the author at jsant@zirkel.us.

With my deepest gratitude I wish to thank Annie Garcelon, Anne French, Steamboat Writer's Group, Jan and Joe McDaniel, Nancy Harris and my son-in-law, Gary Albright, for all the help they provided me to produce this book.

CPSIA information can be obtained
at www.ICGtesting.com
Printed in the USA
FSOW02n1518190617
35404FS